OUR DANGEROUS BRIDE

TREASURE FALLS BRIDE #4
BOOK FOUR

LACEY DAVIS

A Dangerous Woman with a Bounty on Her Head

Francis Nelson is considered armed and dangerous and wanted by the law after robbing the Orangeburg, South Carolina, bank multiple times. But she would do anything to protect her mother and sister, including leaving her home to become a mail-order bride.

Alexander Romney and Daniel Smith made enough money as bounty hunters to purchase their ranch. Always just one step on the right side of the law, now they're trying to live a good, clean life until a dark-haired beauty temps them in ways they never dreamed possible and opens the door to the past.

A past they would like to forget, but Francis's secrets follow her to Montana. Coming face-to-face with their enemy, will they have to choose between their past and their wife?

CHAPTER 1

Francis Nelson spurred her horse faster, racing down the road. The posse was not far behind, and while part of her wanted to ride through the trees, one wrong move and you could lose your head.

Her horse was starting to tire and she hated that she was riding the animal so hard. But when the law was on your tail, you had to run.

"Come on, girl. We're almost to the turnoff," she said, knowing if she could just reach the hollows, they would never find her. She turned down the hidden lane and quickly took the trail that was the back entrance to the house. During the war, they had used this little hideaway often.

Slowing her horse, she reached the barn. Lather dripped from Sadie's sides. Jumping off, Francis rushed the horse to the inside of the barn, knowing they weren't out of danger yet. At any moment, the law could be closing in.

She untied her saddle and pulled out the sack of money. Not a lot, but enough to keep them from going hungry.

Her sister Lilly raced into the barn. "The law is riding up. Hide."

"Shit," she said. "Release Sadie and let her go free. I think I about ran her to death."

They released Sadie out the back of the barn and Francis slapped her on the hind end. The mare took off, but she wasn't running. The horse wasn't dumb and she disappeared into the trees.

Oh God, Francis hoped Sadie would survive because she loved that horse, but today, she'd given her all.

"Hide, they're at the house," her sister said urgently.

Francis opened the underground cellar door and slipped inside. Her sister covered the door with a blanket and then scattered hay.

"Miss Nelson," she heard a voice call.

"Back here," her sister said cheerfully. "I'm cleaning out the horse stalls."

Francis would be surprised if Lilly knew how to clean a horse stall. Between the two, her sister did more of the cooking. And none of the outside work.

The law had never gotten this close. Of course, as soon as she stepped out of the bank, it seemed like they were waiting for her. And the chase had been on. Racing through the streets, down the road, and out of town, she'd clung to Sadie fearing at any moment they would tumble and be captured.

If they caught her, she would surely hang because the law didn't give women bank robbers a break.

Stepping back as far into the depth of the cellar as she could, she heard three men walk into the barn.

"Where's your sister Francis?"

Lilly turned and smiled. "Who wants to know?"

"I'm Sheriff James Randolph and these are my deputies," a man said. "We need to speak to Francis. We think she's the person who's been robbing the bank."

Lilly started laughing. "You men been drinking? My sister Francis is one lazy woman. Why do you think I'm out here in the barn taking care of the horses? It's because she refuses to. Most of the time, she's in town having tea with some of the other women."

"Tell me which ladies," the sheriff said. "I want to verify she's having tea and not withdrawing cash."

Oh, very clever man. Francis had never attended a tea. The Nelson sisters were not invited. Since the war, they lived on the edge of poverty, their names were never mentioned when there was a party of any kind.

"I don't know who. If I did, I would tell them not to invite her. She needs to be here with the rest of us cleaning horse stalls, chopping cotton, canning, and doing the wash. Things a young woman should never have to do, but since Papa died, we're managing."

The man was silent for a few moments before his voice became gruff. "Look around out back and see if she's hiding."

"Do you know how to clean horse stalls, Sheriff?"

"Of course," he said.

"Well, if you're going to stick around then make yourself useful. I need to finish up and then tend to all that laundry hanging on the line. If that lazy sister of mine would stay home, all this work would get done."

Oh yeah, she was so lazy. She was the one holding up the bank so they had money to pay the taxes on the place and also put food on the table. Until the next harvest came in, things were going to remain tight.

Their fortunes had not improved.

"Sheriff," her mother called, "I think I found something you might want to see."

Her mother had no idea what was going on. Not long after their father's death, it was like she woke up in a different world every day. At night, she kept waiting for their father to come home. If Francis went to jail, she worried what would happen to her mother and sister. They were all barely surviving.

And Momma, bless her heart, continued to wait for their father to come home.

Lilly began to hum a tune while she cleaned the stalls. Acting like she didn't have a care in the world when so much was at stake.

Her mother's screams pierced the air. "Stop. Don't touch me or my husband will kill you."

Shouting came from outside and Lilly dropped the pitchfork and hurried from the barn. Sitting there in the darkness, it was all Francis could do to keep from jumping up and running out the door to see what was happening.

"You son of a bitch, what are you doing?" Lilly cried.

"Can't you see something's wrong with her? She's an old

woman," Lilly screamed. "Leave her be. She knows nothing. She barely even knows she's here."

They were trying to draw Francis out of hiding. And it was working. Another minute of this and she'd come out fighting.

"You tell your sister this time we only tied up your mother. If she doesn't turn herself in within twenty-four hours, we'll harm your mother and you. We know she's the bank robber and she's got to pay for what she's done."

Normally, Lilly would have cursed them, but all Francis could hear were sobs. What was she going to do? She couldn't let them harm her remaining family. Maybe she should just walk out of the barn like nothing had happened.

But she was still wearing her men's clothing. They would easily recognize her as the bandit. If they caught her, she would hang.

"Get off our property," Lilly said. "And don't come back. My sister is not a bank robber. Now get out of here before I grab my gun."

CHAPTER 2

*T*he sun had set and the moon had risen in the darkened sky. All afternoon, Francis had paced the small cellar where her sister insisted she stay, fearing the house was being watched.

The dingy room smelled of horses and she'd been tempted all afternoon to open the door and walk out, but she feared for her mother and sister. The law had already hurt her mother, what would they do tomorrow?

It had to be after midnight as she sat across from Lilly, a dim lantern on the table between them.

"You've got to leave," Lilly said, her eyes filling with tears.

A pain seized her gut and traveled up her spine. How could she walk away from them?

"No, I can't go off and leave you to take care of Mother. You'll starve," she said, fearing everything that was going to happen tomorrow when the sheriff returned.

As much as she hated to, she would turn herself in. What choice did she have?

"And if you stay, they will hang you," Lilly said. "Do you think our mother could survive watching them do something so horrible to her daughter? She can't deal with Papa's death and knowing that you were going to hang would kill her."

Francis took a deep breath. Bank robbing was not an occupation she had wanted. But then neither was whore and that was about her only other choice. Their small farm could not produce the money they needed to survive.

"Look, I was in town a couple of days ago and found this flyer. It seems like the perfect solution," Lilly said, handing her the piece of paper. "I was considering it, but you go. I'll stay here with Momma."

Glancing down, she knew that her sister was right. She had no intentions of marrying anytime soon, but this could be a way to get out of town and leave her bank-robbing career behind.

Montana was thousands of miles away and the thought of leaving everything she loved was terrifying. Damn the war and damn her father for getting killed not long afterward.

"But that would mean I would have to leave you and mother behind," she said softly.

"That's better than hanging," Lilly replied. "Look, this is not good, regardless, but you were only trying to keep us from starving."

It was true. She'd never planned on robbing a bank, but when your belly was empty and your stomach gnawing on your insides, and your family was just as bad off, you took matters into your own hands.

You robbed a bank.

She glanced at the flyer. "This is in Charleston. How am I supposed to get there?"

Lilly shook her head. "You need to leave tonight because there is no telling what time they'll be here in the morning to catch you. Take one of the horses. Not Sadie, but one of the other ones. It will take you two days to reach Charleston and then you'll hopefully be free. Sell the horse."

Desperation had her reaching out to Lilly as she grabbed her arm.

"What about the two of you? What is going to happen the next time you run out of food or the taxes come due? Who is going to take care of you and mother?"

She couldn't leave them. But she would do them no good by being hung either.

Hanging her head, Lilly sighed. "That lawyer in town has been wanting to court me, but I keep refusing. I think I'm going to take him up and hope that he'll take Momma as well. He'll have to or we won't be getting hitched."

An ache filled Francis's heart at the thought of leaving everything and everyone she loved. If her sister married, that would help their situation. She could also sell the farm.

"Oh, I don't want to do this," she told Lilly. "No, I need to stay here."

"You don't have a choice," Lilly said. "If you stay, they will hurt Mother and me until you come out of hiding. If you do, they're going to hang you."

Laying her head on her arms, Francis cried. "They may still do that. You told them I wasn't here earlier today and look what they did to Momma."

"In the morning, I'm going to Patrick, the lawyer, and ask that he come and stay with us until the law realizes you're not here."

With a sigh, Lilly stood. "I've made enough food for you to take with you. We'll sneak you into the house and you can pack a small bag. But you've got to leave tonight. Now."

The thought of traveling in the dark terrified Francis. She'd never traveled far alone.

"Don't make a fire or cook anything. Just ride until you're too tired to continue and then sleep until first light. You're going to need to stay off the main road. Once they realize you're gone, they will be searching for you."

It was dark. It was late, and she was going to be forced to leave everything.

"Come on, as much as we both hate it, you've got to get out of here," Lilly said.

For a moment, they stared at each other in the dim light and then threw their arms around each other and cried softly.

"I'm sorry," Francis said.

"No, you kept us from starving. You saved the house and now because of your bravery, you must leave," Lilly said, sniffling. "I'm going to miss you."

Francis released her sister and dried her eyes. She knew what she said was true, but that still didn't mean it didn't hurt.

"Come on, I want to tell Momma good-bye and I need to grab the things I can take with me."

"And don't you dare write to me because knowing that Yankee-loving sheriff, he'll be watching our mail," Lilly said. "I'm sorry, Francis."

"Me too."

CHAPTER 3

*A*lexander Romney swayed in the saddle as his palomino horse followed the cattle they were moving to another section of the ranch. The mountain peaks in the distance were missing snow, but in just three months, they would be covered in white.

While it was often challenging living in Montana with the blizzards and the cold, bears, mountain lions, and coyotes, it was the only place he wanted to live. Here was the place he and Daniel had settled and bought their ranch, built a house, and were slowly growing their herd.

"Hey, where's your head ?" Daniel asked. "Are you dreaming about those women coming to town?"

Daniel Smith, his friend and half-owner of Paradise Ranch, took off after a calf that was wandering too far from the herd. Racing his horse, he yelled at the cow and guided her back into the fold. Turning his horse, he rode up beside Alex.

"Now, where were we?"

"You were asking me if I was dreaming of pussy. Oh hell, yes," Alex said, laughing. "Every night. Every day. Maybe even twice a day. Aren't you?"

Daniel glanced off at the horizon. His friend wasn't as excited about the ladies coming to town as Alex and the rest of the men were. His friend thought and worried too much, instead of just anticipating what was headed in their direction.

"There's nothing more satisfying than having sex," Daniel said. "But that includes marriage, commitment, a family. I didn't come from a good family."

Alex understood his worries. He had good reason to be concerned. But Alex wasn't worried. They would do whatever it took to be successful. He was certain.

"Do you want me to be the only one to bed our wife and just let me be the father of our children? That doesn't seem fair. And if something happens to me, then who is going to take care of our woman and my children? You?"

Their horses trotted along behind the cattle and occasionally they would have to call out *yeehaw* to keep them moving, but they were getting close to where they would spend the rest of the summer. They had moved the cattle about as high in the mountain ranges as they dared. Not unless they wanted the coyotes to feast on the newborns. And even now there was no guarantee the wild animals wouldn't take their calves.

"That's not what I want," Daniel said. "If we have a wife between us, there is no way I'm going to be able to keep my hands off her."

"And we both know that eventually, she'll be with child, and that baby will be one of our sons or daughters."

They had discussed this problem many times, and no matter how often Alex told him it wasn't a problem, Daniel still worried.

"Man, your family is about as wild and crazy as they come. But you've changed your name. You're no longer involved with them and you're different. Until we bought the ranch, you were chasing their ass and arresting them. Now you're a good guy. As long as they stay away, I'm not concerned."

Daniel frowned and shook his head. "I know, but I worry that somehow their bad blood will come out in one of our sons or daughters. What if they grow up to be an outlaw? How would you feel knowing your son or daughter was out stealing from people?"

Alex shrugged. "No problem. I'd haul his ass off to jail. Or even worse, shoot him."

For a moment, Daniel stared at him in shock and then he started laughing. "You are one cold-hearted son of a bitch."

Alex didn't know if he could shoot someone he loved, but he knew he could make them think he would. And Daniel was right, he could be a cold-hearted son of a bitch if he had a good reason.

"No," Alex said. "I'm a law-abiding citizen who use to be a bounty hunter. I'm not going to put up with that nonsense. Not even for a son or daughter of mine. I don't see a problem. You're worrying too much. Stop putting the evil eye on our future children. Instead, start thinking about all that pussy we're soon going to be enjoying."

Another cow began to wander in the wrong direction and this time Alex clicked his heels against his horse's side and he went after the straggler.

"Get on back there," he yelled at the slow-moving animal.

Another half mile and they would be at the grazing fields where the herd would finish the summer. The errant cow jogged back to the herd.

"Now stay there," he told her as she mooed at him.

His horse trotted back toward Daniel.

When he caught up with him, Daniel grinned.

"What if there is not a single woman that arrives that we want?"

"I would say you are being way too picky. Surely, out of eight women, there will be one that takes a liking to two handsome cowboys with big dicks."

Daniel roared with laughter. "You're so damn confident."

Why wouldn't they be confident? They were good men with a nice spread and a newly constructed house that had two extra bedrooms besides their marital bedroom. Any woman would be lucky to have them for husbands.

"Of course, I am," Alex said. "This is what we waited all these years for. It's finally our time. We have the ranch, now we need the woman to spread between us. Then eventually, we'll get the little ones. Our own family."

A sharp pain speared his chest at the thought of his family. They were good people. Damn good people who had been taken from him much too soon.

"You have it all planned out," Daniel said.

"Not me, *we*," he said. "And don't you dare chicken out on me now. We've been waiting for years for this opportunity."

In Kansas City, they'd met and started working together. Not long after that, they shared their first woman, a whore. It was then they began to dream big. A ranch, a family, and most of all, a woman between them.

So when they learned that Treasure Falls, Montana, was a place where there were two men for every woman, they eventually made enough money to end their bounty hunting days and moved here.

Now they owned Paradise Ranch. When the town started talking about ordering mail-order brides, they quickly signed up.

Soon, very soon, their brides would be arriving. And their bachelor days would come to an end.

"I'm not going to chicken out on you, but I'm going to be cautious. I don't need my criminal family to suddenly come to life in the children we create with our bride. It would be devastating to all of us."

"You're damn crazy. Stop worrying about how our children are going to turn out and focus on the wife we're soon going to have. I'm hoping she has either dark or red hair. A curvy waistline and legs that are long and lean that she will wrap around me. I'm hoping her pussy is tight - she's a virgin. And we make her ours."

Daniel laughed. "Yeah, that's enough to make my cock spring to attention."

"Focus on that," Alex said, his own cock hardening at the thought of plunging deep into his bride's willing cunt.

They arrived at the gate, and he open it for the cattle to stream in.

"Fatten up," Alex called. "The bigger you are, the better."

Daniel chased after some strays that wanted to go the wrong direction. He and Daniel were lucky, damn lucky, to be living their dream. All they needed was a woman to finish it off.

Alex glanced around at the clear blue sky. Though in some ways he wished he'd never met Daniel, most of the time he was glad.

The man's family were criminals and Alex hated every one of them. What they did in Kansas City had been wrong. And almost all of them had paid the price. But there were a few who slipped out of town before being caught.

As long as that family stayed away from Montana, Alex was fine. If they came near him, they were dead.

CHAPTER 4

*F*rancis cried as she rode down the road away from her family. Bless her heart, her mother had not understood the good-byes. She thought Francis was going off to school and admonished her for dallying.

"You're going to be late," her mother told her. "Now go. You know that teacher doesn't like you being tardy."

"Yes, Momma. I love you," she said hugging her, knowing they would never see each other again. How could she walk away from those she loved?

Running from the room, she gave her sister one last hug, knowing she couldn't even write to let her know she survived.

"You must go now," Lilly said, tears rolling down her cheeks. "I don't want to see you hang."

With Francis's heart splintering inside her chest, she stepped up into the saddle and slowly rode down the lane away from the house. Her sister stood inside crying in the dark so no one would think they were up. If they were watching the house from the front, she was safe. But if they were watching the back of the barn, they would see her ride off. And she would soon know when they rode after her.

The first fifteen minutes, she kept waiting for them to surround her. But there was no sound of horses' hooves behind her. The second fifteen minutes, she heard the sounds of the dark and that terrified her.

Her sister had warned her to go as far as she could tonight before she rested. When the sun came up, the law would be searching for her.

It would take her two days to reach Charleston. Two days of riding almost nonstop. And it would be a miracle if she made it there without them catching her.

The sound of the bushes rustling had her kicking the sides of the horse. She couldn't go too fast for fear of the poor animal tripping in a hole, but what if there was a coyote or a bear or even a mountain lion in the woods?

The horse picked up its speed and they rode on in the darkness. The moon occasionally would light up the road, but mostly they just rode. Finally, after what seemed like forever, when her eyes were no longer focusing, but drifting closed, she pulled into a clearing.

When the horse came to a stop, she sat there waiting, listening to make certain no one rode behind her. When she felt she was alone, she stepped down from the saddle.

Ground tethering the horse, she pulled out her blankets and made a pallet on the grass, praying no snakes were close. A log lay near her and she moved it to where if she needed the limb, she could reach it.

Plus, she wore a small pistol strapped to her leg beneath her petticoats.

The day had been overwhelming and exhaustion had her eyes closing. Just as she drifted off, she heard the noise. A horse.

The hoof beats slowed and she realized whoever rode that animal was stopping.

Reaching beneath her skirts, she found her pistol and quietly pulled it out of the holster. Her hands were shaking beneath the blanket and she feared she'd shoot herself.

The horse came to a halt and she knew she'd been found. Her heart pounded in her chest and she tried to keep her breathing steady and calm when she wanted to leap up and scream.

In the darkness, she watched a man dismount and walk toward her. She pulled back the hammer on her pistol and waited.

He leaned over her in the darkness and she recognized his face. The sheriff. And then he laughed.

"Francis Nelson, bank robber. You're under arrest," he said as he knelt beside her and grabbed her arms. "But first, I'm going to take what I've wanted from you for a long time. You're a stuck-up southern belle who probably let who knows how many southern soldiers between your legs. And I aim to take advantage of your whoring ways. You're going to get some Yankee cock."

The pistol was beneath the covers and he was holding her arms. She tried to kick him, but between her skirts and the blankets, her legs floundered beneath the covers.

"That's right, fight me. That way, you'll make it even better for me. I like it when a woman doesn't want what I'm about to give her. You're about to get the best eight inches you've ever experienced."

Fear filled her and she knew she was not only going to be arrested, but the sheriff meant to have his way with her.

Leaning over her, he pressed against her, shoving his cock between her legs and she almost gagged.

His lips covered hers, the smell of tobacco nauseating. He tried to push his tongue into her mouth and she bit him.

"You little bitch," he said rising up, releasing her, giving her the opportunity she'd been waiting for.

She jerked the covers out of the way, revealing the gun pointed at him. His eyes widened and she fired the gun, hitting right below his shoulder.

"You bitch," he screamed.

The close range of the gun had her ears ringing, but she was still fighting.

His arm hung useless and then he slapped her with his other hand.

"Get off me," she yelled. "Or I will shoot you again, but this time I'll aim for your head. Do you understand? Or maybe that eight inches you want to give me."

With his good hand, he went for the gun, twisting her wrist until she heard it snap. Screaming, she kicked him, she punched him with her good hand. With her fingernails, she tried to go for his eyes, but he pulled back at the last second.

Blood continued to trickle from his shoulder while they fought. Finally, she remembered the stick of wood lying behind her. Reaching back, she grabbed the branch and brought it down on his head.

Wham!

She hit him as hard as she could.

The man slumped on top of her.

Her heart was pounding in her chest as she pushed and shoved the big man off her. He rolled over onto his back and she scrambled up. Her wrist was throbbing and she ripped a piece of her petticoat and wrapped it around her wrist.

Though it continued to throb, it no longer flopped about. In the darkness, she searched for her gun. When she found it, she reloaded the weapon and put it back into her stockings.

Then she gazed at the man lying sprawled in the dirt.

She laid her hand on his chest and could not find a heartbeat. He was dead.

"Dear God, I killed him," she cried. "No, no, no. I only wanted to stop you."

Killing a law enforcement official was the worst crime she could have committed. Now they would definitely hang her. Now they would search for her until they found her and then she would die.

Squatting, she cried. This wasn't fair. He'd been trying to rape her and she fought to save herself, but she also knew that a jury would find her guilty. No one would believe a bank robber who only wanted to save herself from the sheriff.

She should give up and turn herself in. Her life was over. Sitting there, she sobbed for the life she wanted. The life she would never have. The life this man had taken from her. She cried until she realized the darkness was fading.

No time for tears. She dried her face and got up. She would live these last days to the best of her ability. Her time here on this earth would not be long, but her final days would be the happiest she could make them.

And that meant going on to Charleston. That meant going for as long as she could until they caught her. Then she would hang for her crimes.

But until then, she would live as happily and normally as she possibly could.

Covering the body with her blankets, she did her best to make him appear sleeping, and just as the sun was rising, she got back on her horse and continued on her way, staying off the main road.

No one would know he was dead until later today. She had a few days before they found her and hauled her off to jail.

CHAPTER 5

*T*he next morning, Francis arrived in Charleston. She rode her horse to the livery stable and sold the animal to the man there. No, she didn't get much for the poor animal, but at least now she had a little cash to keep her going.

Until they found her.

Then she went to a secondhand dress shop and purchased a dress that was nice and didn't have blood stains on it. Quickly, she changed right there in the shop and then shoved the dress under a pile of brush to be burned out behind the store.

Now she was ready to face the bridal broker. And she hoped she wasn't too late.

Hurrying down the street, she averted her eyes and kept her head down as she searched for the address on the flyer.

Walking up to the door, she knocked.

A tall woman answered the door and Francis gazed at her. She held up the flyer. "I'm here to become a mail-order bride."

The woman smiled. "Come in dear, what's your name?"

"Francis," she said, not really wanting to give her real name. Knowing that any day now wanted posters would be put up all over town.

"Ida Newton, matchmaker," she said.

Francis hesitated before entering the house, wondering if this was as safe a place as she could get.

"When are we leaving for Treasure Falls?"

"Dear, I need one more girl. Hopefully in the next few days." The woman held the door open for her.

With one last glance at the street, Francis entered the house.

"Can I stay here until we leave?"

The woman smiled. "Yes, dear. But I have to ask. Are you a virgin?"

Thank goodness, she'd stopped the sheriff, though she'd had to kill him. "Yes."

The woman reached out to shake her hand.

She would not be leaving again until they left for Montana. Her next steps out of the house would be to go to the train station. And there, she hoped she would be able to leave her fear behind her here in Charleston.

"Oh my, what did you do to your hand?"

Francis hated lying, but she had no choice. "I fell on it."

"Have you had a doctor look at it?"

"No," she said, thinking she did not want to risk going back out in the street.

The woman stared at her for a moment. "How about if I have the doctor come here and take a look at it."

For a moment, she hesitated. But the darn thing had been hurting.

"Thank you, that would be great," she said. "I did it last night and it's been aching and is swollen."

"We need to have someone look at it before you start on that long trip. Now let's fill out the paperwork."

Just then a beautiful woman waltzed into the room. "Mrs. Newton, I must complain."

She saw Francis and stopped, her eyes going over her hair, her face, and her dress. Her brows lifted and she sighed. "Another one?"

"Yes, Alice meet Francis," Ida said.

"No last name?"

"My last name is Little," she said lying. "Francis Little. What about you? No last name?"

The woman gave her a snarly grin. "Alice Burns. The Burns of Atlanta."

"Oh, that town that burned during the war," Francis said. "Did your plantation go up in flames?"

The girl's eyes darkened and Francis realized she'd probably just made an enemy, but she'd been snooty and condescending, and after last night, she wasn't going to accept being mistreated. Her life had been cut short and there was no need to accept mean, nasty people.

"It burned to the ground," Alice said and turned on her heel and strode out of the room.

Mrs. Newton shook her head and muttered. "Two more

days. Two more days." The woman turned back to her. "I'll send for the doctor while you fill out this paperwork. Then I'll show you to your room. I'll put you in with Blanche. She's a sweet girl who lost her home."

Francis could certainly relate to that. It was the reason she robbed the bank. To pay the taxes that were overdue.

Just then Francis heard a group of horses ride down the street. Mrs. Newton walked over to the window and glanced out.

"Oh, my," she said. "Looks like a posse in search of someone."

Francis felt her heart skip a beat and she realized they were searching for her. Soon there would be posters everywhere showing her face.

She glanced at Francis. "Let me show you to your room. Then I'll send for the doctor."

Francis reached out and touched the woman on the arm. "Thank you for taking me."

The woman smiled. "Soon you'll be in Treasure Falls, Montana, with a husband. Then you can thank me."

But she couldn't then. Because if Francis made it to Treasure Falls, she would never be able to contact anyone she knew here.

As she walked down the hall, she took a deep breath. She'd made it this far, only a couple days more, and she'd be safe.

Two days later, Francis sat on the train, a hat covered her face and she gazed at the city of Charleston. She'd made it. She was going to Treasure Falls, and as long as she made it to the territory of Montana, she should be safe.

A tear trickled down her face as she thought of her mother and her sister. Someday, she hoped she could write them, but not now. Not for at least ten, maybe even, twenty years from now.

CHAPTER 6

*D*aniel stood with the other men waiting for the stage to come in. It was a big day in Treasure Falls and yet he wasn't certain he really belonged with this eligible group of bachelors. They were miners, ranchers, bankers, and even the mercantile owner was here. All of them searching for a bride, hoping that a woman got off that stage that attracted them, and yet Daniel feared he wasn't good enough.

Without a good start, a man often took a wrong path. Daniel had been raised by a family who didn't believe in law and order or even working to earn a living. They survived by stealing, threatening, and killing people.

He'd witnessed his first killing at age eleven. They had inducted him into the family business by smearing the dead person's blood on him. The memory was disgusting.

At the age of eighteen, he'd walked away, determined he would find a way to survive without blood on his hands.

Alex walked up and pushed a man. "Get out of my way. We've been here all morning waiting."

One thing about Alex, he was always short on patience, but he was determined to come out ahead. And you didn't want to be the person standing in the way of his wants or needs.

Alex turned to him and grinned. "I think I can smell pussy already."

Daniel shook his head. "Watch your language. There are ladies present and that is not the way to court a woman. Even I, backwoods man that I am, know better than that. Women don't like that kind of language."

The man shrugged. "You're right. But I'm so excited. Think about how long it's taken us to get this far. From the streets of Kansas City to now has been a few years. A few years where I had to keep you on the straight and narrow."

There had been times Daniel was tempted to return to a life of crime. It was his pattern. It was how he was raised, but he also had seen his family members be killed or hauled off to jail.

That was not the life he wanted. Was it wrong to want to live a normal life like everyone else? To have a family that didn't hide every time a lawman rode up? Who were not looking for their next victim?

It wasn't until he was an adult that he realized that not all families stole, cheated, and murdered to make their living.

"Oh, that you did. But I liked making more money than my family by catching criminals and turning them in. It seemed like a fitting occupation for a boy who they swore to kill if I came around again."

Alex turned and smiled. "We were a good team, but I'm glad those days are over. Now I want a wife, a couple of kids, and enough cattle to make a decent living without having to find bad guys and bring them to justice. Here, the only thing looking to kill us are mountain lions and bears."

It was true. Their lives as ranchers were so tame compared to hunting down men wanted for killing. And now Daniel didn't want to ever step on the wrong side of the law again.

Those days were long since over. Now he worried about passing down his outlaw tendencies to his children. For that reason, he wasn't certain he wanted to never have children and yet he knew that Alex wanted a family.

That was the reason for them being here today. To find a woman who would marry them.

Aunt Grace, the woman in charge of the brides stood off to the side. She glanced at the watch pinned to her dress. "The stage normally arrives at two p.m., but it could be late today."

"Stage is coming." A cry came from a man closer to where the coach would unload cried out.

Sure enough, Daniel saw the two stagecoaches coming around the bend into town. Time to find a wife.

Aunt Grace jumped up and down like a teenager. "The women are arriving. Get ready men. Be on your best behavior and don't act forward. Anyone who does will have to answer to me."

Like he would answer to the older woman. But then she

and the doctor were the ones organizing this along with the nephews.

"Men, line up. The women will walk down and you'll get a chance to meet all of them. Remember first impressions are very important."

"Are you ready," Alex said, excitement in his voice. "This is what we've been working toward."

Not really. But Daniel knew how important it was to Alex. Would a woman accept a man like Daniel who came from one of the most famous criminal families in the U.S.?

The men began to yell and wave their hats as the stage pulled to a stop. The driver set the brake and then he slowly climbed down the steps until his feet touched the ground.

Daniel couldn't help but wonder how much gold, if any, he had on that stage. In his old days, his family would have come charging into town and held everyone up. While several held the gun on everyone, the others would collect their cash. One person would be going through the stage to confiscate anything that looked of value.

It was odd that he still had thoughts of how his family liked to rob. But no more.

The driver opened the door and the first woman stepped out of the stage. No, she wasn't his type. Beautiful, but not the woman he wanted.

When everyone had disembarked from the first stage, they began to unload the second.

"How many women are here?" Alex said his hands on his hips as he stared at the ladies.

"Who knows," Daniel said trying not to overreact. What if there was no one for them? What then?

The first few women said hello as they walked by and they were both polite. But none of them excited him.

Then he saw her step off the stage.

"Look at her," Daniel said. "Her waist is small enough, my hands would probably reach around. And all that dark hair."

"Damn, she's a beauty," Alex said. "Let's see how she acts when she meets us."

They stood and watched as the beauty walked down the line of men, smiling and saying hello.

When she reached them, she smiled and it was all Daniel could do to keep from picking her up and carrying her home.

And he was the one who was uncertain about them finding a woman.

"Hello, gentlemen," she said.

Her wrist was in a cast.

"Hello," Alex said.

"Are you all right? What happened to your arm?"

She smiled. "I'm such a klutz. I tripped and fell, breaking my wrist. It's been three months now, so I'm hoping the doctor here will take the cast off."

"What's your name, klutz?" Alex asked her.

She laughed.

"I'm Francis Little from Charleston," she said.

"Daniel Smith," Daniel said, touching her hand, but not wanting to shake it, because of her injury.

"And I'm Alexander Romney, but my friends call me Alex," he said.

"Alex, that's a beautiful name," she said. "Daniel, the lion tamer."

"Oh no, ma'am. I haven't tamed any lions," he said. "But we do have mountain lions in these parts."

She smiled at them, her large sapphire eyes twinkling with merriment. Oh yes, this was the one he liked the best so far. Even his cock was rock hard and standing at attention.

"Gentlemen, I look forward to getting to know you," she said before she was encouraged to walk on.

The two men turned and glanced at each other before another woman came down the aisle.

"She's the one," Alex said.

Daniel wasn't ready to agree, but right now, all he could do was think about how it would feel to have his arms wrapped around her body and his cock deep inside her.

"You may be right," Daniel said as they welcomed the next woman.

CHAPTER 7

For the first time in months, Francis felt safe. When they got off the boat and were told to take the stage, she knew she was in safe territory. No one would ever find her here. Or so she hoped.

And with her new last name, she didn't think anyone would recognize her as Francis Nelson, Bank Robber/Murderer. She had yet to see a wanted poster, but it was something she feared.

She felt so bad about killing the sheriff, but dang, he had tried to harm her. It had been self-defense. And he'd broken her wrist.

Wiggling her fingers, she thought it was healed, but maybe tomorrow the doctor could take a look and let her know what he thought.

Of all the men she'd met a few minutes ago, she liked Daniel and Alex the best. Daniel with his big brown eyes that seemed to see right through her. His voice was soft, but deep like a gentle rumble. Those full lips were made to be kissed, and she realized she'd not been this excited about a man since she couldn't remember.

And Alex, that man had bad boy written all over him. Dark hair, dark brows, and green eyes just brimming with mischief. She didn't know which one she would choose.

Daniel appeared more of the family man while Alex would be someone to have fun with. Lots of fun. And right now, she needed to laugh and play. Three months of traveling with women had grown tedious. Especially that nasty girl, Alice.

The woman lived to create drama.

Suddenly a loud whistle had her looking around.

One of the men drew their attention to him.

"We're having a supper tonight at Uncle Owen's and Aunt Grace's home at six thirty. For now, we're going to let the ladies get settled in, clean the dust off, and rest before the evening's festivities."

Good, a chance to rest before they were strolled in front of the men again. She needed a chance to clean up and prepare. Because she wanted to get married as soon as possible. The sooner the better.

Aunt Grace smiled and took charge of the gathering. "We have a pig roasting and our cook is making lots of good food for tonight. You are to dress in clean attire to meet these ladies. And of course, we will expect everyone to be on their best behavior."

Aunt Grace walked to the front of the line. "Follow me, ladies."

Unable to resist. Francis turned and glanced at Alex, she

winked at him and gave him her brightest smile. Tonight she would decide which man she wanted to marry. But either of those two would be perfect for her.

Alice walked up beside her. "What a disgusting, dirty little town."

The woman was such a troublemaker.

"I think it's lovely. Just the kind of community I was hoping for. Small, where everyone knows everyone else."

A repulsive noise came from Alice. "Have you chosen which man you want yet?"

There was no way she would tell Alice her choices. Because knowing her, she would go after whatever anyone else wanted.

"Oh no," Francis said. "There are so many great choices and I want to see which one would fit with me the best."

Alice appeared disgruntled. "I'll accept no one except the banker or the mine owner. Everyone else is just so below my standards. I mean miners. Who wants to marry a man who spends all his time in a hole digging for gold or ore."

Francis wished she would walk somewhere else. All she needed was for the men to hear Alice's remarks and for them to think she felt the same.

"I'm just so thrilled to be here. It's a great chance to begin again and find love and happiness."

"Begin again? What are you talking about?"

Oh, no, she'd let it slip and somehow she had to get her attention off what Francis had said.

"You know. Moving away from a place that is still trying to

recover from the war. Losing my home. Just a new beginning. That's what I was looking for."

When they walked inside, Aunt Grace divided them into two people per room. Thank goodness Francis stood close to Blanche and she was going to room with her. Anything to get away from Alice.

"Ladies, dinner is at 6:30. Wait up here and we'll call you all down one by one. We're so thrilled you're here. Tonight, I hope you meet a man who fulfills all your dreams. Now get some rest."

The women all walked into the bedrooms and Francis lay on the bed. "A soft bed. I'm so happy to be here."

"Me too," Blanche said. "And I think I found a man I really like."

"Who?" Francis asked.

For the next hour, they sat on the bed and talked about the men they'd met and how they couldn't wait for tonight.

CHAPTER 8

*A*lex stood with all the other men waiting for the women to descend the stairs. His mind was made up and he knew what he wanted. His cock also knew what he wanted and was standing at attention knowing that soon there would be the one woman he wanted in the room.

An elegant, beautiful woman who he could hardly wait to get to know better.

"Down, boy," Daniel whispered. "You look like you're ready to jump on her the second she comes down those stairs."

"Don't want any other man to grab her. She's going to be ours," he said confidently, knowing he'd do whatever it took to get the woman he desired. And he wanted Francis.

Daniel laughed. "You're going to scare her."

"No, I'm going to make certain that no other man in here tries to take what's ours."

In some ways, he felt like his inner male was just ready to

pounce on the poor woman. His cock was hard, his breathing shallow, and it was like he could smell her womanly scent.

"But what if she doesn't want us? What if someone else caught her fancy? What are you going to do then?"

A chuckle rumbled from deep in Alex's chest. "Not a problem. She's going to want us. Only us."

"Damn man, you're so confident, you're cocky," Daniel said.

"That I am," Alex replied. "Look, here they come."

The first few women came down and the doctor had them stand on one side of the room. That wouldn't last long. Then there she was at the top of the stairs. He looked around ready to knock anyone out of the way who got out ahead of him.

Like a princess, she floated down the stairs in a dress that he couldn't wait to remove from her curvaceous body.

He and Daniel blocked the other men and stepped in front of her.

The doctor frowned at them and motioned them to go back to the other side, but they ignored him.

"Gentlemen," she said with a smile, "I'm happy to see you."

"We'd like to escort you to the table," Alex said.

"I'd love that, but first we have to wait until after the doctor speaks. I'll see you soon," she said and floated to stand next to the other women.

Just then the doctor cleared his throat. "Welcome, ladies, we're so glad you're here. Tonight is a chance for all of you to get to know one another. The men will tell you who their partner is so that you'll get to know both of the men at once. You have two weeks to make up your mind before we will have a wedding ceremony right here in the house. You'll marry one man and the other will be your second husband."

Alex grinned at Francis who appeared surprised.

"Two men? Did he just say two men?" she mouthed.

There was chatter among the women.

"Excuse me. What are you saying concerning two husbands?" one of the women asked.

The doctor suddenly appeared stunned.

"In Treasure Falls, there are two husbands for each woman. We have lived this way for many years due to the shortage of women. This way if one husband is killed, the second man is there to make certain the family is taken care of."

Francis's mouth formed the perfect O and he wanted to lean in and kiss it closed but resisted. Aunt Grace would not appreciate him kissing her in front of everyone. But later tonight, he intended to take advantage of the situation.

Jesse walked up beside his uncle. "This has been our way since Treasure Falls began, for many different reasons. It's not a bad way to live. You have a legal husband and also a second man who will love and take care of you."

The women were all gazing at one another. Obviously, the marriage broker had forgotten to mention this very important detail. And yet, Alex was enjoying their beautiful, shocked expressions.

How many would be on the next stage back to Charleston?

Some looked like they were ready to run. He glanced at Francis and she smiled at him. Oh, that's what he wanted. A woman who was not afraid. A woman who would accept the situation.

Aunt Grace moved to stand beside the doctor. "Ladies, I've lived this way all my life and my husbands have kept me very happy. Sadly, Silas died last year. So now it's just me and the doctor."

The room grew quiet, filled with tension as Alex could see the women choosing what to do.

"Did the matchmaker not mention this?" Jesse asked.

"No," the women cried.

"I'd like to know more about this way of life. I'd like to talk to Aunt Grace in private sometime. We have two weeks before we have to make a decision. I'm willing to consider having two husbands," one of the brides said.

Her words seemed to calm the women. The others nodded in agreement.

The woman who spoke, Alex didn't know, but he admired her spunk. If he wasn't so committed to Francis, he would have considered her. But his eyes were on the dark-haired beauty standing across from him and Daniel.

Slowly, one by one, the women agreed that they were willing to take a chance and learn more about their lifestyle.

He gazed at Francis wondering if she was willing to take a chance on having two husbands. "What do you think?"

The woman tilted her head in a saucy manner that had him longing to run his tongue up her neck as he bent her between him and Daniel. But that would have to wait.

"I think you should take me outside to the patio area, get me a glass of something to drink, and we should figure out if we're a good fit." She smiled and gave a little laugh. "Two men. Now I don't have to choose between you. Now I can have both of you."

Damn, this woman was making him hot enough to set off fireworks. There was a reason he had chosen her. A damn good reason. He liked her spunk.

The men grinned at each other, and before another man had the chance, they each took her arm and led her outside. She laid her hand on the inside of each man's arm and gazed up at them, her sapphire eyes sparkling.

It was all Alex could do not to lean down and kiss her, but he feared one would not be enough.

Two women were standing at the corner, and he could see they were upset about the news of two husbands. "Who is that?"

One of the ladies walked away shaking her head.

"Alice Burns," Francis said. "If she's your type of wife, then I know we'll never be compatible."

Daniel lifted her good hand to his mouth. "No, she's not who we're looking for. You are."

"We picked you out this afternoon," Alex said. "Now we just need to get to know one another."

Her stunning eyes twinkled with laughter as Daniel pulled out a chair for her at a small table. Then he walked off to get them a drink while Alex sank down in the chair next to her and leaned on his hand, staring into her gaze.

"Tell me about yourself. I want to know all the details," he said.

"Not much to tell. My papa was killed not long after the

war and we've been struggling to survive ever since. I finally gave up and decided to head west when I saw the flyer for mail-order brides."

She leaned into him and reached out to touch his arm. "How does it work with two men as your husbands?"

This woman was curious and Alex couldn't wait to show her exactly how two men worked, but he also didn't want to frighten her. Still, she had to know the truth.

"Not much different than one man, only now you'll have both of us at the same time."

"But how?"

Reaching out, he took her hand. "One of us will claim your pussy and the other will claim your ass. We'll take it slow and get you accustomed to both of us, but eventually we'll take you at the same time."

Her face flushed and she gasped.

"Will it hurt?"

"Not if we're doing it right. Your pleasure will always be important to us. If we don't have you screaming with desire, we're not good lovers. And, honey, I can promise you I'm a very good lover."

A smile crossed her face. "I've never considered whether or not my husbands would be good lovers."

Just then Daniel walked up and set their drinks on the table before he sat.

"Obviously, I'm missing some very interesting conversation. Is Alex promising you he's a great lover?"

She laughed. "Yes."

Daniel picked up her hand and brought it to his lips. "I

don't have to brag. Your happiness and gratification are a certainty I guarantee. By the time I'm done with you, you'll be begging me for more."

Francis glanced between the two of them and smiled. "I've never experienced this pleasure you're so certain I will feel. I have nothing to compare it to."

Alex stood and took her hand. "Come with us."

They took her just outside the lights of the house and Alex leaned her back against Daniel.

"Put your arms around Daniel's neck," he commanded.

Daniel's palms came around to her front and he caressed the front of her dress, her breasts fitting in the palm of his hand.

Alex knew what he wanted, but he wasn't certain she would let him. His lips covered hers as his mouth took possession of her mouth and she moaned against him. His tongue swirled around the edges of her lips and then he dove inside. When she tried to pull back, he ground his hips against hers, letting her feel the rigid hardness of his cock.

Releasing her lips, his mouth trailed down her neck to her chest. Quickly he pulled her breast out and laved her nipple with his tongue.

"Someone's coming," Daniel said quickly.

Alex nipped her nipple with his teeth before he shoved her breast back into the bodice of her gown.

They moved to either side of her and Alex smiled into her dazed expression.

"That's just a sampling of the satisfaction you'll receive," he said, turning to the side as people came out the door.

No one needed to see the bulge in his pants.

"What do you think?" Daniel asked her. "Are you prepared to be loved by not one man but two?"

Turning her head, she glanced at each man. "When can we get married? The sooner the better."

CHAPTER 9

*L*ater that night as they rode their horses in the dark toward their ranch, Daniel couldn't help but think about the woman they would soon marry. He'd had his reservations before she arrived, but now these two weeks could not pass quick enough.

"Do you think I should tell her about my past?" he asked Alex.

"Only if you want to," Alex said. "We really need to court her some, so we can all learn about one another. I'd hate to marry a woman and then learn she has secrets she didn't tell us about."

"Kind of like our secrets," Daniel said.

Would a woman as refined as Francis want to marry a man who came from an outlaw family? A man who even now had a cousin terrorizing the Midwest with bank robberies?

Would she want to marry the son of a gunslinger and a whore? His family was not an example of piety and good behavior. Lawlessness was their claim to fame and also the only way they knew how to make a living.

"After we're married, I'm going to insist she learn how to use a gun. What if we're out and your family rides up or some other criminal," Alex said quietly. "Anyone who touches our woman is a dead man."

That was a fear that Daniel lived with all the time. When they gave up bounty hunting, they had moved as far from Missouri as they could. Many of his family he had arrested and taken to jail to collect the bounty on their heads. Many of them hated him.

It was why he'd changed his name and moved to Montana. To begin life again without his criminal family finding him.

"After we're married, I'm going to enjoy removing her clothes and spanking that creamy white ass of hers," Daniel said, thinking of how she would look draped over his knee.

Alex moaned and rubbed his hand across his cock.

"I've been hard all day. The very thought of all that gorgeous dark hair hanging to the floor as we spank her or even surrounding my cock as I shove it into her mouth has had my balls strung so tight. She seems willing and ready."

Daniel laughed. "I couldn't believe I walked up to the table and you guys were talking about sex."

"She asked me how it works with two husbands."

Daniel thought about how Francis had responded to their kisses in the garden. There was so much more he had wanted to show her but knew that someone could walk out at any moment.

"Does it seem like she's really going to enjoy sex?" Daniel asked.

"Yes, and I'm so glad. I don't think I could have taken a woman like that Alice Burns who got all upset because she'd traveled all this way only to learn she would have two husbands."

Daniel shook his head. "I would have taken her across my knee if that had been my woman. Right there in front of everyone."

Alex chuckled. "Yeah, me too. I wonder if Francis realizes we're going to spank her ass."

"No, she seems innocent. I don't think she understands what we're going to do to her."

They rode along, their horses plodding toward their ranch. The moon high in the sky lit the way.

"That's why I think we need to take her on a picnic and give her a sample of what is about to happen to her."

"But we can't have sex with her," Daniel said. "We're not going to take her unless she's our wife, and then hell, we may do it on the sidewalk in front of the church."

Alex started laughing. "That would certainly shock everyone. But I bet the doctor is going to marry us and we'll just need to leave as soon as possible."

Swaying in his saddle, Daniel knew he was getting tired and they were still a good mile from the ranch. The land they had purchased was far enough away from town that hopefully the community would never grow out far enough to reach them.

Also, far enough away from the mining so that they didn't

have to put up with the noise and the construction. Mining was hard work and he never wanted to get involved.

As excited as he was about Francis, Daniel still had reservations about having children. "I'm going to do my best not to get her pregnant."

Alex shook his head in the darkness.

"Oh, good grief. Believe me, no child of ours is going to get involved with criminals. I'll do everything I possibly can to keep them from leading a life of crime."

That was so easy for him to say, but Daniel was afraid. How could an entire family be involved in criminal behavior? Was it something in their blood?

Sometimes Daniel felt like he must have been adopted because he was different from the rest of them. Sure, he was headed down that path, and then his father committed a horrible crime that disgusted him and he walked away.

Even today, it made him sick to his stomach.

The moon shone down on the road as they came around the last bend. A coyote howled in the distance, the sound lonely and haunting sending a chill down Daniel's spine.

"Some things are out of our control. My family dying while I was gone was out of my control. Your uncle's actions were out of your control. Some things life just doesn't let us make decisions on. Having children with Francis is out of your control."

That made perfect sense, but Daniel was still going to do his best to make certain that he never fathered a child. And yet he knew that he wanted Francis badly. He also wasn't stupid.

It would be very hard to know which man fathered a child with Francis. But that still didn't mean he wouldn't stop trying to keep from getting her pregnant. There were ways and he would do his best to make certain that she didn't bear any children from him.

Because he feared his blood was cursed blood that preyed on other people.

Just then the horses turned down the lane to their house. They were home. And tomorrow, they were going to take their bride on a picnic.

One where she would learn more about what happened between a man and a woman.

CHAPTER 10

Francis had never felt so drawn to two men in her life. Daniel with his dark sultry looks that sent a tingle up her spine before it delved into her middle, causing her to feel so warm and achy.

Alex with his deep laugh and the way he gazed and spoke to her made her breathless. And the man's kisses had been hungry for something she didn't understand. The sheriff had tried to kiss her, but she'd been revolted at the feel of his mouth on hers, but Alex she wanted, needed, more.

Today, they were picking her up and taking her out to the countryside for a picnic. And she couldn't wait to see them. She couldn't wait to kiss them, deeply without prying eyes.

The first month on the trip here, all she had done was cry. Missing her mother and her sister. The second month she'd become so afraid glancing at everyone on the boat, wondering which one would soon arrest her.

The third month, she'd made a vow to herself to stop

worrying and live. When the stage pulled into Treasure Falls, she'd known that this was her new beginning. This was her chance at a life filled with love and happiness.

"Good morning," Daniel said, walking into the house. He came over and kissed her on the cheek.

"Good morning," she said with a shy smile, determined that today she was going to have a great time with her two new men.

"Good morning," Alex said, glancing around and then dropping a quick kiss on her lips.

She laughed. He was the one who threw caution to the wind and did whatever made him happy. While she enjoyed Daniel's steadfastness, she longed for Alex's recklessness.

"Are you ready to go?" Daniel asked.

Today, she wore one of the dresses she'd bought at the secondhand store. It was yellow with a full skirt, a sweetheart bodice, and puffed sleeves that only covered her shoulders.

"Let's go," she said, glancing around at the women who sat in the house waiting for their men to show up.

Taking her by the arm, they hurried out the door and down the steps of the big house. Alex helped her up into the wagon while Daniel walked around and got in on the other side of her. She sat between them, both of their thighs close to hers.

"It's about an hour's ride from here to the ranch," Alex said. "But we'll get you back long before dark."

Daniel clicked to the horses and the wagon began to roll.

"Tell me about your ranch," she said, truly interested in the place she would eventually move to.

"We have two hundred acres that we run cattle on," Daniel said.

"Our home is a two story that we just completed back in the spring. It has three bedrooms, a kitchen with a hand pump, and a nice living area with a big fireplace to heat the house in the winter."

The thought of living in such a nice house made Francis smile. Her family's farm had been small and the house only had three rooms. But that was her past and this was her future.

"Do you have any goats?"

"No," they both replied.

"Didn't want any," Daniel said with a chuckle.

Alex laughed. "We do have some chickens, though the damn coyotes keep getting into the hen house."

"Oh no," she said. "My papa finally created a trap that caught the coyote that was bothering our chickens."

It had been so many years ago and yet here she was sharing it with these two fine men. Glancing at them, she longed to run her fingers down their arms and feel the muscles beneath their shirts.

"Tell me something about living here that you enjoy," she said.

Alex frowned. "We'll have to take you to the falls. You'd enjoy that. It's beautiful and has a legend that is interesting."

Daniel glanced down at her. "The peace. The tranquility. Watching the sun come up over the mountains in the morning while I sip from a hot cup of coffee. Makes me feel at peace."

Reaching out, she touched Daniel's arm. This was what she enjoyed about this man. The way he expressed his feelings. Each man had unique qualities, but Daniel had a soft heart and she just wanted to curl up in his lap.

There was no doubt he would make a wonderful father.

With a smile, he gazed into her eyes and she felt like she would melt under the heat of his intense look.

"You have to know, that I didn't want to get married, but Alex did."

"Why not?"

"My family is not exactly the kind of people you want to marry into," he said. "They're heathens to say the least."

"Oh," she said. "So why are you marrying me."

"Because there is something about you I just can't resist."

A grin spread across her face and warmth filled her. There was something about Daniel that drew her to him. Alex as well, but Daniel seemed to reach in and just grab her heartstrings and yank them to him.

"I also love the winters. Especially since we'll soon have a wife to snuggle with," he said staring at her like he couldn't wait to remove her clothes.

She had not thought about the winters. It must get really cold here. And she had no winter clothes. None. No coat, nothing.

"What are the winters like?" she asked gazing at Alex. "I'm sure they must be cold."

The stare he gave her had her heart racing. "It can get downright frigid. We'll need to get you some boots, a heavy coat, but no women's long johns."

"Why not?" she asked, puzzled, thinking that was what she would need the most.

"Because our woman will not be wearing underclothes. We want you available to us at all times."

For a moment, she let that sink in and then she realized he meant sex. She would be available to them whenever they wanted to bend her over a desk, a chair, or just drop her on the floor and have sex with her right there.

Was this how married people lived? She was so confused.

"All right, but what if I get cold?"

They both laughed. "Honey, we're not going to let you get cold. We're going to keep you warm."

Alex grinned at her. "Darling, anytime you get chilled, I'll be right there to warm you up."

This just seemed surreal.

"But what happens when we have children? You can't just bend me over a table and take me right there in front of them. That's not right."

Daniel smiled. "When we have children, we'll be a little more discerning. But that's probably a year away. And between now and the time our children are old enough to walk, we're going to take you whenever we want. And I can't wait."

Suddenly her mouth felt dry at the very thought of them using her this way. And yet, it didn't sound bad. She licked her lips and when she did, Alex reached up with his hands and pulled her mouth to his.

His lips became demanding, taking control, and heat blossomed up from her center. A moan escaped from between her lips and she seemed to melt under the intensity of his kiss.

"Damn, next time you're driving," Daniel said. "It's my turn to kiss her like that."

A bump in the road had them breaking apart.

She reached up and touched her swollen mouth.

Yes, her mother had explained to her what happened between a man and a woman, but she'd never talked about the feelings, the emotions, the desires that a man's kiss could evoke.

She'd never mentioned the rush of heat between her legs. The way she wanted to lean into Alex and let him continue to make her feel so good or the desire that exploded within her.

"How much farther," she asked. "Daniel deserves a kiss and I want to make certain he gets one."

The man smiled at her. "Darling, don't worry. I planned on taking you just as soon as I stop the wagon."

"I would have been disappointed if you hadn't," she said and she meant it. Daniel had not had the chance to kiss her like Alex, and she couldn't wait to explore his lips and see how he tasted. How his kiss was different from Alex's.

Five minutes later, Daniel pulled the wagon to a stop. "We're here. This is the back pasture. We don't want to compromise your reputation, so we're going to wait and show you the house after we're married. But we'll be all alone here. There's no one around."

There were big trees on the edge of a huge field that had cattle munching on the grass. As she gazed at the scenery, she felt Daniel's big hands on her face.

"My turn, darling," he said as his lips covered hers.

His kiss was gentle. His kiss was not as demanding, but the way he held her, she felt cherished, wanted, and she relaxed into his embrace and let him hold her. With his mouth, he expressed so much tenderness and emotion that she clung to him, wanting more.

It was then she realized that she was going to have the best of both worlds. One man who was curt and demanding and took what he wanted and a man who was gentle and sweet and treated her like a queen.

Daniel eased out the kiss and gazed into her eyes. "You're ours. If you have any questions or doubts, you need to raise them now. Because after this picnic, we're not walking away. Do you understand me?"

Well, maybe her gentle giant did have a demanding personality after all. He was letting her know they were serious about getting married and if she wasn't, she needed to walk away now.

Only problem was her past and she hoped it stayed in South Carolina. Francis Nelson was dead and Francis Little was going to live a happy life here in Montana.

"Yes," she said, knowing there was no one else she wanted. Only these two men would make her their wife.

A grin spread across his face and he jumped out of the wagon and reached back to help her out.

"I'm starving," Daniel said.

Alex reached into the back of the wagon and pulled out a picnic basket that was loaded with all kinds of goodies, including a bottle of wine. Daniel grabbed the blankets and they took her by the hand and led her to a spot by the tree.

After they spread the blanket, they pulled out the food, opened the bottle of wine, and enjoyed the food the cook had prepared. Francis kept looking around at the scenery. It was beautiful here and this would be where she lived.

Leaving South Carolina had been the best thing she could have done for herself.

"What made you decide on this place," she asked.

"Because it's beautiful," Alex replied.

Daniel smiled. "It's quiet and there are no people around."

That was for certain and that could only make her feel safer.

When they were finished, they each lay back on the blanket and gazed out at the mountains.

"It's stunning here," she said, knowing that the day was quickly slipping away.

"Honey, we want to give you a taste of married life. Just a small taste," Alex said, rising above her.

What did he mean?

"We're going to wait until we're married before we show you everything," Daniel said rolling over to her. "But we all deserve a little taste of what is to come."

"Take off your bloomers," Alex commanded.

"What? Why?"

Why in the world would they want her to remove her bloomers?

"Because I told you to. Today, you're going to experience your first orgasm."

A nervous flutter filled Francis's stomach and yet she wanted to do what they said.

Daniel helped her as she lifted her bottom, reached beneath her skirts, and pulled down the undergarment. With a yank, he took the garment from her and brought the bloomers to his nose.

In shock, she stared at him.

"Sweet, sweet pussy. But you won't be needing these any longer."

"Why not?"

"Because you're no longer going to wear bloomers or any type of undergarments. You will always be available to us, anytime, anywhere we want to take you."

They had talked about this in the wagon. Now she understood what they wanted. And yet she was not prepared to have sex with them today. Not until they were married.

"We're waiting until we're married," she said as they moved over the top of her.

Once again, she knew she was in a perilous situation, but she wasn't afraid. These were good men who would never hurt her.

"We're waiting, you're not," Alex said.

He took her hand and laid it on his cock and she gasped. He was hard. Very hard. Gazing up into his face, she saw the desire shining from his eyes.

"I did that?"

"Yes," he said.

Knowing that she caused his penis to be hard filled her

with a power she'd never experienced before. She liked that feeling. She liked knowing that she excited her men.

Daniel unbuttoned the bodice of her dress and pushed the undergarments to the side. She felt his fingertips on her flesh as he pulled her breast out.

In amazement, she watched as he lowered his head and brought his lips to her nipple. A tingle zipped through her straight to the apex of her legs and she gasped. Both men were making her feel so very wanted. So very good.

"I'm going to lick you from top to bottom," Alex said as he moved down her body and raised her dress, exposing her very naked womanhood.

For a moment, she panicked and tried to close her legs. "What are you doing?"

"Oh no, darling, you're going to love this. Lie back and enjoy. Let me look at you. Taste you."

Alex spread her legs wider as his head disappeared between them. He kissed his way up her leg and she tensed the closer he came to the apex of her thighs. She cried as she felt his lips on her womanly folds. His tongue licked her, sending strange sensations through her body. Heat sizzled and crackled along her spine and her breathing became raspy.

Daniel was suckling her breasts and Alex was creating a firestorm between her legs.

A flood of sensations spiraled up through her body and she opened her legs wider, needing something more.

"Alex, what are you doing? What's happening to me?" she asked, her breath rushed.

"Relax," Daniel said "You're about to have your first

orgasm. You're safe. We'll take care of you. Just let your body take over and it will carry you."

Her hands clenched the blanket and she could feel the tension gripping her. "Oh no. Oh, no. Please."

Something was happening to her and she didn't know what. A rush of tension gripped her as her world seemed to tilt.

Daniel's lips covered hers and his mouth was demanding as his tongue swept inside her mouth. Clinging to him, she clutched his shirt as his lips overtook hers.

She couldn't breathe. She was drowning as a wave of desire engulfed her and she broke the kiss.

"Daniel," she cried as her body arched up off the blanket while Alex continued to lick her, the firestorm growing. It was like he had a magic tongue that was making her lose her mind.

Her body tensed and her breathing became a gasp for air.

"Alex," she cried.

"Ride it, baby, ride it," he murmured against her.

Then the explosion inside her took her over the edge and she screamed as she closed her eyes. A million stars filled her as she tensed her body shaking with a vibration she'd never experienced.

It felt like she had fallen over a cliff and was slowly floating back to earth.

For a moment, she lay there not moving, spent, as she slowly ebbed back to the blanket beneath the big beautiful blue sky.

With a sigh, she opened her eyes, feeling drained and surreal. What had just happened?

The sun warmed her as she gazed at her two men. They stared at her with the biggest smiles and she knew they were proud of what they had done here today.

"Your introduction to sex. The rest will have to come after we're married," Daniel said.

But that wasn't what Francis wanted. This introduction had made her want to know everything.

She wanted it all. She wanted to know what it would feel like with them inside her. She wanted to know what it would feel like with one of them taking her ass. She wanted her men, now.

And yet they were breathing in a slow measured way like they were trying to control themselves.

"Why are we waiting?" she asked. "Fuck me, please, fuck me."

Daniel shook his head. "I'm sorry, darling, you've got to wait."

"No," she cried. "I want more."

Alex grinned. "Believe me, it's even harder for us. But we have to wait. Two weeks and then we'll be married. Then we'll take you every way we can."

With a sigh, she knew there would be no more pleasure from them today. And two weeks seemed like forever.

CHAPTER 11

*A*lex couldn't wait for today's adventure. When they took Francis on the picnic, she'd been responsive and eager and begged them to fuck her. It was the hardest day of his life and he'd spent the evening relieving himself thinking of how many different ways they were going to take her on their wedding night.

They had waited a couple of days to let them all recover before they went on another picnic.

But today they planned to take her to the falls and maybe even take a dip in the water. It was hot and the water would be cool.

Alex drove the wagon while Daniel sat beside Francis, holding her hand, occasionally kissing her and the man even fondled her breast once they were out of town.

"Tell me about the falls," she said, breathless from Daniel's kiss.

"There was an Indian warrior who loved the chief's daughter. But the chief didn't think he was the right brave to marry her. So he told the warrior if he could find the lost treasure of the Absaroka Range, he could marry his daughter. The old chief didn't believe in the treasure.

"The warrior loved the girl and he searched for months, finally, he came back and told the chief that the treasure was in the falls near Helena. The chief didn't believe him and refused to let the warrior marry his daughter. The two ran off. The chief had the warriors in his tribe go after them. When they were about to be captured, the couple confessed their love for one another and dove into the falls together. They died in each other's arms. Now you can sometimes see the faces of your dead loved ones there. The legend of Treasure Falls."

Alex loved the expressions on Francis's face. Her mouth dropped open and she gazed at them. "Really? You can see the faces of your loved ones?"

"Sometimes," Alex said. "I think it's a bunch of bull. I've never seen the faces of my dead loved ones."

Just thinking about them caused his chest to ache with pain. Maybe today he would tell Francis about his family, but then again, why ruin a perfectly beautiful day? He would much rather spend it in her arms. Her wet arms.

Turning the horse, the wagon pulled onto the lane that led to the falls. You could hear the water tumbling over the rocks into the pond down below before you saw the falls.

"Watch for animals," Alex warned.

"Animals?" Francis asked.

"The deer, elk, bear, and even a mountain lion like to drink at the pond," Daniel said.

As they came around the curve, there was the water. Alex gazed around the area but saw nothing.

"Looks like we're alone," he said, bringing the wagon to a halt. After he set the brake, he jumped down and reached up to help Francis alight.

Leaning in close to her, he took a deep breath and then he kissed the side of her throat. She wrapped her arms around his neck and pressed her body against his.

"All right you two, we should eat before we indulge ourselves," Daniel said.

Alex leaned back and shook his head. "Don't listen to him. He's been kissing you all the way out here and now it's my turn."

She giggled and laid her head on his chest. "Kiss me all you want, Alex. I like it."

Did the woman know what it did to him when she said things like that?

With a growl, he covered her lips with his and drank from her mouth like a starving man needing nourishment. With a nip on her lips, he broke the kiss, but let his lips trail down her neck, her chest to the top of her bosom.

"You smell so good, I could just eat you up," he whispered.

"Go right ahead," she said. "I'd like that very much."

Daniel made a noise. "The food is ready."

Slowly Alex pulled himself away from her bosom and glanced at his friend. The blanket was spread and the food had all been put out.

"Daniel wants to eat food. I'd rather continue eating you," Alex said.

Francis gave him a saucy smile. "Maybe we should eat. I think you're going to need your strength."

His cock hardened. Oh yeah, he was going to need his strength to keep from taking her completely. She was such a tempting little morsel that he wanted to devour.

Grabbing her by the hand, he led her to the blanket where she sank down beside Daniel.

The little temptress reached over and kissed him. When she released him, she smiled. "Didn't want you to feel left out."

It was ten days away before they could marry and Alex wasn't certain he would not explode with need before then.

"Thank you, darling," Daniel said and then handed her a plate.

"Where's mine," Alex asked.

"Fix your own," Daniel said. "I'm not your maid."

The two men grinned at one another and Alex took some of the chicken and deviled eggs and put them on his plate.

"Do you have any brothers or sisters?" Daniel asked.

"I have a sister. Lilly. I miss her so much, but she is going to marry a lawyer in town. She'll be just fine," Francis said. "What about you boys? Any siblings?"

Alex didn't want to talk about his family. Not now. They were happy, why bring everyone down?

"Not anymore," he finally said.

"Oh, I have them spread across Missouri, but they're not important," Daniel replied.

Her brows drew together in a frown and Alex knew that

she wondered why they were not important. He didn't want to talk about things that were not happy. He didn't want this day to be ruined.

The sun was shining bright and the rays were warm.

"Let's go swimming," Alex said.

"I don't have anything to swim in," Francis said.

"We're going naked," Daniel replied. "But you can swim in your chemise."

Alex could see her feeling awkward.

"Come on, darling, I'll help you get undressed," Alex said.

"Wait," she said, holding up her hand. "We're not going to do anything until we're married, right?"

The woman wanted to make certain they were not going to have sex.

"That's right," Daniel said. "But, honey, it doesn't hurt to look does it?"

She licked her lips nervously. "You men tempt in ways I've never considered before now. No, I guess it doesn't hurt to look. But when you touch me, I just about lose my mind."

Daniel chuckled. "I'm glad."

"Me too," Alex said. "Now stand up and I'll help you undress. You didn't wear bloomers did you?"

She grinned. "No, you told me not to."

The woman was learning. But, damn, the idea of pulling her across his lap and spanking her had been such a temptation.

"Good," Daniel replied.

Slowly she stood and turned her back to Alex. Quickly he unbuttoned the dress and slid it down her arms.

Next, he undid her corset.

"Throw this damn thing away," he said.

"I can't. Not until after we're married. Then we'll burn it," she replied.

Alex didn't agree, but he wasn't going to argue with her, but as soon as they said I do, the contraption was gone.

She stood before them in a white cotton shift. As soon as she was wet, they were going to see everything.

"Come on," Daniel said taking her hand. "Let's get in."

Alex glanced over to see his friend as naked as the day he was born. His cock stuck out in front of him like a weapon. Francis's eyes trailed down him and she smiled.

Obviously, she liked what she saw.

Quickly Alex shed his clothes. She took his outstretched hand and together they jumped into the pond. The water was cold and it felt good against his heated skin.

She laughed and then swam away from them. "I haven't been swimming since I was a young kid. Girls are not supposed to go swimming. Especially with two naked men who are not her husbands."

"But will soon be," Daniel replied as he pulled her to him.

Lucky man, he held her tightly and she gasped, wrapping her arms around his neck. "This feels so nice."

"Yes, it does," Daniel said as he began to kiss her wet neck.

Alex swam up behind her, his cock had recovered from the cold at the sight of her swimming across the pond, her wet shift clinging to her.

Her lips were on Daniel's when he pulled her tight against him, his rock-hard cock nestled between the cheeks of her ass.

She released Daniel's lips and leaned back against him, angling her head until she could kiss him. The feel of her warm wet lips against his own had him groaning.

Soon they would be married and he couldn't wait.

He pushed his cock into her cheeks even harder and she gasped.

Knowing he was reaching his breaking point, he swam away. Daniel did as well and she grinned at them. She pulled her clinging chemise down and swam to the bank where she tossed it onto the grass.

Dear God, the woman was as nude as a newborn baby.

She swam away from them toward the falls and then she slowly climbed up the rocks until she was standing beneath the waterfall naked.

Did the woman not understand what she was doing to them? Staring at her creamy full breasts, her tiny waist, and full hips, it was all he could do not to grab her and take her right here in the water.

She was a temptress that he didn't know if he could ever get enough of. And right now, he was fighting the urge to take her before they married.

Suddenly she dove off of the slippery rocks into the clear water. She swam up to Daniel.

"Race you to the bank," she said and took off swimming with Daniel right behind her. With a laugh, she reached the bank before him.

"You had a head start," he told her, pulling her out into the deeper water.

"It was the only way I could beat you," she said with a giggle. "I mean look at these big strong arms."

She ran her fingertips down his muscles and Alex decided he wanted to feel those fingers stroking him.

When he reached her, he lifted her out of the water and carried her onto the grass. She weighed little of nothing, and gently, he laid her on the blanket.

"Alex, what are you doing?" she asked, her sapphire eyes darkening with desire.

"Exactly what I want too," he told her. "The other day we gave you pleasure. Now it's your turn."

A smile spread across her face. "What do you want?"

"Besides wanting to take you right here on this pallet, but knowing I'm committed to waiting, I want you to give me some relief."

She reached out with her hands and rubbed his chest. "How can I do that?"

"Suck me," he said and moved over her until she could take his cock in her mouth. "Run your tongue around the head and then suck it into your mouth. Don't let your teeth touch it. But suck the end of my cock and once I receive my pleasure, then you can do Daniel while I taste your beautiful pussy once again."

A grin spread across her face and eagerly she ran her tongue around the head of his cock, then pulled him into her mouth.

Daniel walked up to the blanket. "Change positions. I haven't had a taste of her pussy yet."

Her eyes widened as Alex moved up so that Daniel could

reach between her legs. Out under the beautiful blue sky, Alex closed his eyes and let the workings of her mouth and tongue ease the ache between his legs. It was a welcome respite until they said their vows and he could shove his cock into her tight pussy.

With Daniel working between her legs, he felt her body tighten. She moaned around his cock, creating a wonderful sensation that tightened his balls. Though he could tell this was her first time, he knew that it wouldn't take long until she could suck his cock into tomorrow in little or no time.

Already he could feel his seed building inside, getting ready to explode. Though he wasn't ready to let go, if she kept manipulating him with her tongue, it wouldn't be long until he exploded into her sweet mouth.

With a groan, he felt his balls tighten. "I'm going to come and I want you to swallow every bit of my come. Do you understand?"

Her sapphire eyes widened, but he could see the desire that Daniel was creating. Her hands reached out and grabbed the blanket twisting it in her grip.

Suddenly there was no turning back, he shoved his cock deep into her mouth, his hands gripping her head as he held her in place as he came. The release was so intense that he threw his head back and groaned.

His limp cock slipped from between her lips and she moaned. "Daniel."

Leaning down, Alex covered her lips with his and his fingers reached for her breasts as he twisted the nipple.

Her hands reached up and grabbed him as her orgasm

ricocheted through her body, causing her to tense and shudder beneath him. A moan escaped from deep in her throat.

As he released her lips, her breathing was fast and quick.

"Oh," she cried. "What is having sex going to be like if it's this good between us now?"

The two men chuckled.

Daniel Francis from between her legs. "Up on your knees."

Gazing at him with a glazed look, Alex moved so that she could do what Daniel requested.

Alex knew what he wanted. They had been with too many women together not to know each other's signals.

Daniel rubbed her buttocks and then he popped her on the ass.

Stunned, she whirled around and gazed at him. "What are you doing?"

"Showing you how it will be between us."

"But you hit me," she said.

"And I will again," he replied. "Anytime you do something wrong, we will spank you. And sometimes we'll spank you just to give you pleasure."

Alex could see that she was confused and he nodded to Daniel as he moved until he was beneath Francis.

Reaching up, he pulled her mouth down to his.

Daniel's hand smacked her, but with his other hand, he found her clit and began to massage it.

A groan escaped from between her lips and he smacked her again.

This time he hit her ass several times in a row.

Alex released her mouth and watched as he spread her cheeks and began to work his finger in her ass.

"Daniel," she cried.

"Relax, honey. I promise you're going to love what I'm doing. I promise before I'm done, you'll come again."

As Daniel worked his finger in her ass, his other fingers continued to stroke her clit. Alex watched as she tried to fight the feelings that were overcoming her. She closed her eyes.

"Francis, open your eyes and look at me. Know that soon I will be your husband. Know that soon, we will both take you at the same time," he told her.

"Oh," she cried as the orgasm seemed to rush upon her.

"That's right, darling, clench my finger. Someday that will be my cock you're clenching."

With a scream, the orgasm overcame her and she shuddered beneath the onslaught of his digits working her.

"Daniel," she cried. "Daniel."

"Come all over my hand," he told her.

With a final shudder, she collapsed on top of Alex and he loved the feel of her satiny skin against his own.

Glancing up at Daniel, he smiled and nodded. Today had been just about perfect. He didn't think it could get any better than this at least until they were both deep inside Francis.

CHAPTER 12

The two weeks seemed to take forever to arrive. Finally, today was their wedding day. Francis could at last feel safe that she would never be found. With a new last name, who would know that Francis Nelson also known as Francis Little, soon to be Francis Romney, was ever a bank robber? Or murderer.

Life in Treasure Falls with her two very handsome soon-to-be husbands had been better than she ever thought possible. Even now, the thought of being discovered was terrifying because then she would lose the men she found herself falling in love with.

Yes, this was different from anything she'd ever experienced, but it felt right. Already she was falling in love with sweet Daniel who would do anything to make her happy, though he did love to spank her ass.

And Alex, there was a heat burning within him that she knew would probably burn their house down tonight when they finally had sex. It had been building for quite some time and she was so ready to experience the feel of them inside her.

Already she'd learned that each man was different. Each man made her feel unique and beautiful and she couldn't wait for them to consummate their marriage.

Aunt Grace had taken her into the office and explained to her how her husbands would prepare her for both of them to take her. It had been a candid discussion and she told her not to be frightened. That having two men at once was a beautiful experience.

Now Francis stood there waiting for her name to be called to walk down the stairs and join her husbands.

Walking out her door, Aunt Grace stood by the stairs. "Oh, Francis you look so beautiful. Good luck."

"Thank you," she said. "And thank you for helping me to understand."

The older woman smiled. "Tonight will be a wonderful night."

And Francis believed her. She wasn't afraid of the wedding night or the marriage bed. In fact, she was eager to experience whatever lay in store for her. Alex and Daniel had already shown her how beautiful it could be between them.

As Francis descended the stairs, she smiled at the two men waiting for her. They were her men and she was honored to be their wife.

When she reached their side, Alex kissed her on the cheek and whispered. "You look so beautiful."

"Thank you," she said, her heart pounding with excitement.

Daniel locked her arm with his. "I'll always remember this day."

She smiled at him. "You told me you didn't want to get married."

"Honey, I would have married you as soon as you stepped off that stage," he whispered back. "You're exactly what I wanted."

His words filled her with warmth.

"And I can't wait for tonight," she whispered.

"Honey, stop, or we won't be staying for dinner. We'll be leaving as soon as the ceremony is over."

She reached out and patted his shoulder. "The sooner, the better."

The doctor stood before them and cleared his throat. She glanced up at Alex and winked at him. Wouldn't they be surprised when they arrived at their house and she wore nothing but her wedding dress? She remembered their words and she wanted to make her men happy, so today, she'd done as they requested.

She was naked beneath the dress.

As the doctor said the words, inside her head, she said a little prayer that they would live their lives with no interference from the law. No reminders of how she'd robbed banks and even shot and killed the sheriff.

That was the past, and oh, how she wanted it to stay there.

Nothing to take her away from her men. That they would have many children and she would be a good mother to her little ones. A family of her own was all she'd ever wanted in life. But she was also loyal to those she loved and she would do whatever it took to make certain they didn't go hungry.

Even robbing a bank.

Suddenly the ceremony was over and Daniel pulled her into his arms and kissed her thoroughly. Then Alex took her and his kiss had her blood sizzling along her spine, clear down her middle.

"More of that please," she whispered against his mouth.

Alex chuckled. "Later. There will be a lot more of that later."

The couples were led outside where long tables had been set up. The dinner went on and on with lots of toasts to the happy couples. Francis was so ready for it all to end. She felt so grateful to the doctor and Aunt Grace, but she was ready to see her new home.

Finally, the couples started to leave.

Though she had remained aloof from the rest of the women, she hated to see them all leave. It was hard to be close to people when you were afraid that at any moment you were going to be yanked away and hauled off to jail.

She hugged them all good-bye, even that witch, Alice, who had caused all kinds of trouble. And it seemed like Alice had chosen to return to Charleston. Well, they could have her.

When she reached Pearl, she whispered in her ear. "Good luck. You know where to find me if you need me."

Pearl was in a lot of trouble with the gambling hall owners and she feared they would follow her here if they learned her location.

And Francis knew she would help protect her if Pearl needed her.

"Thank you, Francis. Here's to a new life," she said softly.

"You too," Francis replied. Though she had not told Pearl about why she left South Carolina, they shared a common bond. But Francis's hunters were the law. While Pearl's were the gentlemen clubs and gambling halls.

Pearl and her men walked away.

Her husbands carried down her small carpet bag that held only two dresses.

"Is this it?"

"That's all," Francis said with a smile. After she'd discarded her undergarments, there was a lot more room in the bag.

A grin spread across Daniel's face. "Let's go home, wife."

"Yes, let's," she said as she took Alex's arm as they left the house.

"Bye," she told Aunt Grace. "Thank you for everything."

"Good luck," Aunt Grace said as they walked out the door.

It was time to start her new life as a wife and hopefully soon, a mother.

Alex all but ran her down the stairs toward the wagon. "Let's go."

"I thought maybe we might go by the cafe and have dessert," she teased.

Daniel laughed. "You are dessert, honey."

"Oh, I can hardly wait," she said.

As soon as they were in the wagon, Daniel flicked the reins and the horses pulled them away from the house. They all waved and then he turned down the street that headed out to their ranch.

Once they were out of town, Alex turned to her. "Remove your bloomers."

She smiled and lifted her skirts to show them she wasn't wearing any.

"You obeyed us," Daniel said. "Good girl."

"I knew you'd be pleased."

"Before we reach the ranch, let's talk about what we expect from you," Daniel said.

The sun was beginning to set and she knew it would soon be dark. This wasn't a discussion she'd expected. They had talked about some personal stuff during their courtship, but somehow they had been so busy doing things to one another, they had forgotten to ask what they each expected.

"You'll be naked the first week we're married," Alex said.

Stunned, she turned to him. "What?"

"We want you available whenever we want you," Daniel said. "We may come in from the barn and decide to take you right there on the kitchen table."

"Can I at least wear an apron while I cook your dinner?"

A grin spread across Alex's face. "Yes, you can do that."

"What if we have company?"

Daniel laughed. "People in Treasure Falls know better than to approach the newlyweds' house the first week. They know what's going on."

"You will obey us all the time. If you don't, we will spank you, and no, it won't be that sweet little sexual spanking you received by the falls. This time we will paddle you until your bottom is red."

Francis didn't like this. "I've not been paddled since I was a child."

"Then don't do anything to deserve one and it won't be a problem. We know this area and you don't. There are animals out there that would love to make you their dinner."

The very thought sent a shiver down her spine and she reacted. "I've never wanted to be some animal's meal. But what about chores? What am I responsible for?"

The man grinned at her. "Mainly cooking, the laundry, and taking care of the house. We do have chickens and you might take care of them, once we let you out of the house dressed."

The cooking and cleaning and even the chickens were not a problem. It was just getting to know them better and learning more about her husbands.

"All right, now let me tell you my expectations," she said.

They both turned and looked at her.

"What? You don't think a woman should also have expectations? After all, you are my husbands."

Daniel cleared his throat. "What are they?"

"You will treat me with respect. You will never hit me in anger, not even a spanking," she said. "You will remember my birthday and our anniversary and I'll remember yours. We will always celebrate those days. Supper will be served at five o'clock and it better be an emergency if you're not able to be at the table on time."

The men chuckled.

"Damn, she's worse than my mother," Alex said. "If you were late to the dinner table, you did the dishes."

Francis turned and glanced at Alex, a smile on her face. "Actually, I think your mother is a genius. I like her idea. You've never told me about her."

His expression changed and he nodded his head. "And I'm not going to tonight either. This is our wedding night."

That was odd, but she would respect his wishes. Very soon though she would expect to learn more about his family.

The wagon pulled up in front of a beautiful two-story log home.

"Oh, I didn't know it was a log home," she said excitedly.

"We built it ourselves," Daniel said, pulling the wagon to a halt and setting the brake. He wrapped the reins around the handle. "Your turn, Alex."

"I know," he said. "I'll be there as soon as the horses are taken care of."

Daniel jumped out of the wagon and turned to lift Francis.

Suddenly he slung her over his shoulder like a sack of potatoes.

"Daniel, put me down," she said, laughing.

"No, I'm carrying you over the threshold. It's bad luck to let your bride walk through the door."

Laughing, she tried to hold onto him, though his hand was very near her bottom and all she could think about was him touching her beneath her dress where she was naked. And the smell of him seemed to envelop her and she sighed as a rush of heat warmed her.

Opening the door, he carried her inside the beautiful home and she gasped.

"This is magnificent," she said. "Oh my."

Once they were inside, he let her slide down the front of him and she could feel his hard, rigid cock. Soon that would be inside her and a shiver went through her. She was a little anxious, but she also had already experienced how her men would make her feel comfortable.

She would have several orgasms before the night was over.

"Oh, Daniel, this is beautiful," she said as she gazed at a big rock fireplace that took up one wall with a bookcase on either side. Stairs were at the back of the room that led up to a second floor where she was certain the bedrooms were located.

"Show me the kitchen," she said, eager to see the rest of the house.

"Let's wait on Alex," he said, starting to undo the buttons on the back of her dress. "Though if you're naked, I doubt he shows you anything but his cock."

She shook her head at him knowing that tonight her men were so ready to claim her and she was ready for them to take her.

"Yes, let's wait for Alex. We don't want him to miss anything," she said, moving away from Daniel who grinned at her.

Just then, Alex came in from the barn.

"Show me the house. I love it."

He grinned and walked over to her and took her by the

hand. "There is only one room, I want to show you. The bedroom."

Daniel laughed. "I told you."

Like a flash flood, anticipation filled Francis. "Well, I wanted to see that room as well. I just thought you'd let me see the kitchen."

"Tomorrow," he said. "Not tonight. Tonight is our wedding night and I'm more than ready."

Leading her up the stairs, he took her down the hall to the last room. A sitting area was outside of the bedroom.

"This area is so that if we have kids, hopefully they won't hear your screams of passion or moans of pleasure," Daniel said as he opened the door and led her inside a very spacious bedroom.

The room had the largest bed she'd ever seen.

"Wow, where did you find the bed," she asked.

"We didn't," Alex said. "We made it from the same pine we used on the house. It was made with the idea that three could sleep comfortably."

Daniel was at her back, unbuttoning her dress again. "Time to get naked."

Once the buttons were undone, he lifted the dress over her head.

She wore nothing underneath.

The men stopped and stared.

"You were beautiful that day at Treasure Falls, but today, you look even better here in our bedroom," Alex said.

Daniel began to remove his clothes. She stared as he removed first his boots, then he yanked his shirt out of his waistband. Next came his pants as he dropped them to the floor. "Time to make you ours."

A hot sparkling thrill sizzled up her spine as his words filled her with anticipation.

"Tonight, we start with your pussy, but soon, when you're properly trained and you're ready, we're going to take you in both places," Alex said.

"As our wife, we're going to take you in your pussy, your ass, and your mouth," Daniel explained.

"You've already used my mouth. I can't wait for you to take my pussy, but my ass, I'm a little nervous."

"Francis," Daniel said in a soothing voice. "Relax, we're going to take care of you. We're going to make you feel so good."

Alex took her face in his hands and had her look at him. "We're your men. And we will decide how to use your body. But you will always experience pleasure. It's important to us that you enjoy it as much as we do. We want to make you happy."

She licked her lips and took a deep breath.

"Just talking about this is making me feel like a fire is spreading through my limbs."

"Good, that's what we want," Daniel said. "We want to just look at you, and you know we're going to take you."

"We want you begging us for our cocks," Alex replied.

Daniel's hands were once again, rubbing over her naked skin. A moan escaped from her and he could see her eyes widen as her puckered nipples grew excited.

Unable to resist, Alex reached out and twisted one of her nipples. She moaned and gazed into his eyes, her mouth open.

"Let's shave her," Alex said as he glanced at Daniel.

Confused she asked, "What are you going to shave?"

"Your pussy," Daniel said as he laid Francis on the bed and then moved between her legs.

Who shaved a woman's hair? Evidently her husbands did and yet she wasn't afraid. In fact, she was curious to see what they would do.

Gently, Daniel pushed her back, letting her feet dangle above the floor. He spread her legs, his fingers trailing over her folds. It was better than a tickle, more intense, more enjoyable.

"There is nothing like a bare pussy," Daniel said as she clenched his fingers.

"That's it, darling. A man loves it when his woman squeezes his cock with her pussy. Remember to do that when I'm plunging my cock into you."

Alex handed Daniel the straight razor and a shaving cup filled with lather.

Her eyes widened.

"Please be careful," she said.

The brush landed on her womanly center and brushed against the folds.

"Aargh," she cried as heat gripped her and she clenched trying to hold onto the rush of feelings that centered between her legs.

"Feels good, doesn't it," Daniel said as he swiped the brush between her legs coating her with shaving cream.

Lifting the razor, his fingers spread her as the razor stroked down her center.

"Daniel," she cried filled with a need so urgent, she feared she would move and he would nick her.

Alex stood over and watched as Daniel swiped the hair from between her legs.

"Oh, look at that beautiful pussy," Alex said as he stepped away and yanked his shirt from his pants. Then he removed his belt and laid it on the dresser. She tried to concentrate on him removing his clothing while Daniel continued to use the razor on her.

When Alex moved back to the bed, he was naked.

"I just want to spank that naked pussy," he said and Daniel glanced up at him and grinned.

"Me too," he said. "I'm all done."

"I'm going to taste that clean pussy," Alex said, leaning down between her legs.

She felt him spread her lower lips before his tongue dove inside her. She raised her hips and cried out.

"Alex," she gasped as she clawed the quilt, trying to control the pleasure rocking her. The feel of his tongue had her racing toward the edge. "Oh, Alex. Stop," she moaned.

Alex halted and raised his lips from her center. Then his hand came down and lightly spanked her pussy. With a gasp, she stared at him as heat blazed through her center.

"In the bedroom, never tell us what to do. We're in control," Alex said. "You will call us, sir. We will do whatever we want to you. Anything. But we will always give you pleasure."

Alex spanked her once again between her legs sending heat rushing through her. She raised her hips trying to escape the stinging slaps that had her crying out with need. He spanked her again landing on her clit.

The next time he spanked her clit, she came, shuddering and crying out. He plunged his fingers inside her and pleasure rocked her. Shuddering, she came crying out his name.

"Alex."

"Oh, darling, I think you like having your pussy spanked."

Feeling drained, she gazed at her husband in shock. The feelings of his hand hitting her there had sent her over the edge and that surprised her. Why would being spanked there feel so good?

But it had. And it had not taken any time at all before she was coming.

"Now, we're going to take you," Alex said. "Now we're going to claim you as our bride."

What these men had done to her in the last two weeks was a prelude to what would happen tonight. But she wasn't prepared for the way they made her feel. No one had ever explained to her that she would experience such pleasure that would lead to an orgasm.

An orgasm that left her craving for it again.

Or the way her body responded to their touch. The feel of their fingers on her ass, the feel of their mouth on her clit, or the way that Alex spanked her pussy. She had been unprepared for what they were doing to her and yet already she experienced so much unbridled pleasure where she felt like the earth had spun around and around.

No one mentioned how desire would culminate in a brilliant flash of color and feelings all centered in her middle. No one told her that the woman experienced pleasure just as much as the man.

Now she was about to lose her virginity, her innocence. And she couldn't wait.

Alex kneeled between her legs. "I'm going to take your virginity now. I'm going to claim you as our wife."

"Fuck me," she cried. "Make me yours."

Daniel moved to her side, took her hand, and placed it around his cock. The skin was velvety smooth and he moved her hand up and down his large organ. It was rock hard and the tip was leaking fluid.

She felt Alex's fingers on her clit as he stroked the folds between her legs. A gasp escaped her at the sensations that seemed to explode between her legs.

"I can't wait to fuck you," Daniel said. "I'm going to shove my cock so far in you, that you're going to scream my name."

"Good," she said with a sigh, knowing that he was the softer of the two men and yet she'd already experienced a spanking by his hand out at Treasure Falls.

Of the two, she realized Alex was the more aggressive man and Daniel was the soft and gentler man, though she didn't think for a moment that he wouldn't be aggressive if he had to be. And she honestly, kind of liked it when they were more aggressive.

Alex's cock was at the entrance to her pussy and she tensed knowing the inevitable was about to happen. She was about to lose her virginity.

"Get ready," Alex said as he lay over the top of her.

"Do it," she cried. She wanted to get past this moment and onto the pleasure.

His hand touched her bottom. His finger swirled around the entry to her ass and she gasped at the sensations his touch created.

With one hand on her pussy stroking her clit and one on her ass, she was in the middle of a firestorm raging inside her body.

It was all she could do to keep from screaming, *do it. Just do it.*

On their own, her hips raised to meet him and he placed his cock at her entrance and gave a little shove. She felt her body stretching to accept him and then he hit her maidenhead. With a shove, he drove his way into her body and she welcomed him.

Pain sparked inside her before the fullness of Alex's cock overwhelmed her. She could feel him deep inside her as he paused to let her adjust to being filled with his cock.

"Oh my God, she feels so tight. I can't hold back," Alex said with a groan.

He began to move inside her and she groaned as the tingles filled her body. With every stroke, a fire seemed to grow. A heat traveled from her center up through her middle and she gripped his penis needing him.

"Darling, I'm not going to last long. You're so tight and you're squeezing my cock," he said to her.

"Alex," she said with a gasp. "So many sensations. Your finger is in my ass."

"Yes," he said, shoving it in even farther. "You need to get used to something being in your ass."

She began to move her hips in time with his and he gasped at the way they moved in sync. "Clench my cock," he rasped. "Clench my cock with your pussy."

And she did and the man shoved his penis in her so hard, she screamed. "I'm going to come."

"Come all over me," he said.

With a sudden shove, she felt his seed spilling inside her and her world seemed to explode as she felt her body begin to shake and shudder beneath his. With a cry, she clung to him, wanting and needing him close.

This was so much better than anything they had done before now as she felt herself coming down. Slowly, she felt her body returning back to earth and she still had Daniel's penis in her hand, though no longer did he move.

Alex was on top of her as he raised up and gazed at her. His hand swept away the hair on her cheeks and he leaned in and kissed her thoroughly. His lips moved over her mouth, commanding and sealing her mouth with his.

When he released her, her breath was raspy once again.

"You're ours. Don't you ever forget it," he said as he rolled off her to the side.

Daniel moved in between her legs. "My turn to claim you. To make you mine."

"Please, Daniel. I want to be your wife," she said as she gazed up at him.

And she realized this was how their marriage would be. This was how her men, her husbands, would take her.

"Up on your knees. I want to take you from behind. I want to see your ass. Because when you're ready, I will claim your ass."

Francis crawled up on the bed until she was on her hands and knees. Alex leaned beneath her and she watched as he put his mouth to her breast. His teeth gently nipped at her nipple and she moaned at the heat that cascaded through her from that small nip.

"Soon, we'll take you at the same time," he said, gazing into her eyes before he placed his mouth on the other breast and nipped her again.

Daniel's hands were at her buttocks and she felt him spread her cheeks. She glanced over her shoulder at him as he rubbed her clit between his fingers. "I'm tempted to paddle your pussy again, just for the pleasure, before I stick my finger in your ass."

"Oh," she moaned, the thought of him striking her there causing her breathing to accelerate.

A groan escaped her as she bit her lip at the desire raging toward her once again.

"This time, we're going to do something a little different. Don't you come until I give you permission. Do you understand? Because if you do, I'm going to paddle you and you know how much I enjoy spanking that ass of yours."

"But what if I can't stop?"

"Oh, honey, I hope you disobey."

A tingle of desire spiraled through her. "But you'll spank me."

"With pleasure," he said.

91

Fingers began to probe her backside at the same time he was rubbing her clit. She could feel the desire building inside her, pushing her closer and closer to the edge. The man's fingers were relentless and she tried to move away, to escape the relentless teasing, but he slapped her on the ass.

"Don't move," he whispered against her ear.

"I'm going to come," she gasped out.

"Don't unless you want five licks," he said.

He shoved his fingers into her ass, swirling them around and it was like a bomb went off inside her.

"Aargh," she cried as the orgasm rushed over her, carrying her to the edge of the world, her body shaking beneath his touch.

"Aw, darling, you came," he said, his voice sounding so fake. "Now I have to spank you."

A tremor of fear went through her.

Alex released her breasts and sat back.

Daniel sat on the bed. "Come, lie across my lap with your butt in the air."

"That's not fair, I couldn't stop," she said, crawling over to him.

The man wanted to spank her and she could see that there was no way she could escape this punishment. Would it always be like this? She wasn't certain she wanted to be punished.

This might hurt and she didn't want any more pain tonight.

Glancing at Alex, she hoped to find some support, some help, but he just smiled. Why did she get the feeling that no matter what she had done tonight, she would have been punished?

"Lie over my lap," he commanded her when she didn't move fast enough for him.

With a sigh, she lay down, his cock poking into her hip.

"You will count every lick," he told her. "Since this is your first spanking since we married, I'll go easy on you."

That didn't make her feel any better. Then she felt his fingers tweaking her clit, rolling and pulling the tiny nub, increasing her desire. What was he doing?

Smack!

His hand came down on her ass and she jumped.

"One," she said with a gasp.

Again, his fingers touched her center and even entered her pussy, rubbing her and making her squirm on his lap. Making her want and need him even more.

Smack!

"Two."

Her cheeks were burning, but a warmth seemed to also be spreading through her. One that was not centered on pain, but rather pleasure.

Again, his fingers entered her and she moved her hips to accommodate them even more. A groan escaped her as he gave her even more pleasure running his fingers through her slick folds before they dove inside her. She could feel an orgasm building and she knew she had to control it or face even more punishment.

But would that be so bad?

Smack!

"Three," she moaned.

This time there was less pleasure and yet her body was starting to clinch in anticipation of another orgasm.

Smack!

"Four," she cried louder.

Moving her hips in time to the plunging of his fingers.

"Don't come," he warned her.

Smack!

"Five," she said with a whimper. It was over and yet her need was greater than ever. And she feared she would not be able to control the desire rushing toward her.

"On your knees," Daniel commanded.

"Yes, sir," she said.

"Good girl," he said, rubbing her buttocks as if to help the burn go away and yet that only increased her pleasure.

Daniel pressed his cock into her pussy and she gripped him with her muscles, hoping that soon he would let her come. She knew that it would take very little for her to come again.

His fingers swirled inside her ass and instead of running from the feeling, she leaned back toward the pleasure she felt there. Who would have known that it would feel so good?

"I'm going to fuck you hard. Mark you as ours and then spill my seed inside you," Daniel whispered against her ear. "You're ours, Francis."

"I'm yours," she whispered, the words somehow coming out.

Alex bit her nipple and she grabbed his face, holding him there, letting the pleasure build inside her. Daniel pounded into her, his balls slamming against her as he relentlessly fucked her.

"I'm going to come," he gasped. "You are free to come as well."

That was all she needed to hear. A scream tore from her throat as she clenched her muscles around his cock, her body shuddering as pleasure rippled through her, causing her to almost black out for a moment.

Then she felt Daniel grasping onto her hips, holding her in place as his cock spilled its seed deep inside her. The two of them collapsed onto the bed with Alex beside them.

This was her wedding night. This was her life now.

A sense of wonder overcame her and she gazed at her husbands. "What more is there to learn?"

"You'll soon see," Alex said as he pushed the hair away from her face.

"I can't wait, but I need to rest a little before we do it again," she said.

They both laughed and placed her in between them.

"Soon we will begin your training," Daniel said. "You are ours. Never forget it."

CHAPTER 13

*D*aniel awoke before the sun rose early the next morning. What a night. They had each claimed Francis three times. And she had loved every moment as they both took her in different positions.

It felt like they had only been asleep for a couple of hours, but it was morning. There were animals to feed and eggs to collect.

And there was a beautiful woman lying next to him with full breasts and a pussy that could hold a man's cock snug. It was a new morning and time to start training their wife. Because soon they would both claim her at the same time.

Leaning up on his elbow, he glanced at Alex. The man was beginning to stir.

"Time to wake up sleepy head," he said, leaning down and kissing Francis's bare shoulder. She moaned.

"Not yet," she said. "I need more sleep."

He laughed and pulled the sheet back, exposing her

luscious backside to him. Placing his fingers on her full rounded buttocks, he caressed her flesh and slowly worked his way into her ass.

She tried to move away from him and he laughed. "You're not going anywhere, princess. I'm going to have me some morning pussy."

Moving over the top of her, the fingers on his other hand found her clit and tweaked it.

"A little more of that, please," she said, moaning into her pillow. "I really like it when you do that."

Now they were getting somewhere.

"Oh, Daniel," she cried.

Before she could respond, he raised himself over her and shoved his cock into her wet, willing pussy, coming from behind her.

"Good morning," she said with a sigh. "Oh…"

"Darlin', your pussy is so tight. What a way to start the day," he said as he leaned down and kissed the back of her neck, his tongue trailing down to her shoulder.

The walls of her pussy clenched his cock and his fingers played with her clit as he shoved into her.

"You started without me?" Alex said, rolling over and facing them.

"Early bird gets the first pussy of the day," Daniel said.

"Shift positions. Roll her over on top of you," he said. "I'm going to prepare her ass."

Daniel shifted her until she was lying on top of him, then he shoved back into her sweet womanly center.

"What are you going to do?"

"Focus on Daniel. You'll soon find out," he said as he rubbed her ass cheeks with his hand.

"I think our wife needs to start off the day with a spanking," he said as he slapped her ass.

"Why?"

"Because it makes your pussy wet," Daniel told her. "Do it again."

"Oh," Francis said when she received the second smack. "I'm going to come."

"Not yet," Daniel told her as he felt Alex shove his finger in her pussy, his cock rubbed the digit, lubricating his finger. Her eyes suddenly widened and he knew Alex was playing with her ass. She gasped and tried to look back to see what he was doing.

"Hold her still for a moment," Alex said.

Daniel watched as he slowly inserted the first butt plug into her tight ass.

"Oh," she cried. "What is that?"

"A butt plug. Your first," Daniel said, holding her so she couldn't see what Alex was doing.

"Someday soon, my cock will replace this," Alex told her. "And then we'll take you at the same time."

Daniel watched her face as she tried to adjust to the feeling of the small dowel in her.

"I'm so full," she said.

Alex pulled it out and shoved it back in.

Her eyes widened and she stared at him. "It feels different."

"Each day you'll receive a larger one until you're ready."

"Oh," Francis moaned as Alex moved the plug in and out. "Smack my ass again. I want to see what it feels like."

Alex smacked her on her ass again and she groaned.

"Why does that feel so good when Daniel's cock is inside me?"

The way the walls of her pussy were clenching his cock, Daniel knew he wouldn't last much longer.

"Should I make you wait longer to come?" he teased her.

"No, please," she cried. "I need to come so bad."

"Good, come when I tell you," he said, wondering if she could last that long. With stroke after stroke, he felt his blood building. Alex smacked her on the ass and she screamed, taking them both over the edge.

"Come now," he cried.

With a last thrust, he coated the inside of her pussy with his come. It was then he thought about how he didn't want to come inside her and yet he'd completely forgotten about pulling out before he spilled his seed into her.

They could be creating a baby. A child. Would that child act like his criminal family? Quickly he pushed the thoughts from his mind. Now was not the time to consider what he'd done.

Like an idiot, he'd forgotten to pull out last night and again this morning. If they created a child, it could be his.

Lying there, slowly coming back down, he loved the feel of Francis in his arms. The way her chest was against his and the sound of her labored breathing.

The sun was up and shining in the window when he crawled off her and Alex took his place.

He slapped her on the ass. "Up on your knees. I want to fuck you from behind."

Alex slapped her pussy and she squealed.

"I can't wait for your pussy to grip me again," Alex said as he moved her into the position he wanted.

Alex spread her legs apart, her pussy glinting with moisture in the light.

Shoving two fingers in her, she moaned and raised her hips to meet his every stroke. Knowing Alex loved taking her from behind, Daniel lay back and let him do the work.

"Are you ready for my cock?"

"Always," she groaned as she moved her ass back to receive him.

Alex plunged into her pussy and she groaned as he slapped her on the ass.

Her breathing was labored as she glanced back at him.

"Is that the best you can do?" she said, her sapphire eyes dark with desire as she teased him.

Daniel sat back and laughed as Alex gripped her hips and slammed into her pussy, his hands moving her hips in a rough way. He was pounding into her womanly center.

"Oh, that's good," Francis said. "Much better."

He slapped her on the ass again and she groaned.

"Don't come until I say you can," Alex commanded. "Or I'll enjoy shoving that butt plug in your ass."

A whimper came from her and Daniel could see she was fighting to keep from coming.

"Now," he said. "We'll come together, now."

One last shove pushed her over the edge and she cried out

as Daniel held her in his arms. "That's it," he said, watching her face contort, her bright eyes darkening with passion and her mouth forming that perfect circle that made him want to put his cock in there.

The three of them collapsed on the bed and she took Daniel's hand in hers. "Promise me it will always be this good."

A chuckle came from him and he pulled her in his arms. "Darling, it will always be this good."

Alex rolled over against her back. "And the best is yet to come."

CHAPTER 14

*T*oday they were going to spend the day together since none of them had gotten much sleep last night.

Daniel slipped a handkerchief over her eyes and tied it. "Be still. We have a surprise."

"But I can't see," she said.

"That's the point," Alex told her, laughing at her. This morning she had made them the best breakfast, wearing nothing but her apron. That might have to become a rule. She could only cook in an apron.

Afterward, they had bathed and now were about to go out riding the ranch and stop for a picnic later. Today, they were going to allow her to wear a skirt while they went riding.

But first, they had a surprise.

"We wanted to get you a wedding present," Daniel said up close to her. "Take my hand and we'll lead you to the present."

"I didn't get you anything," Francis said a little panicked. "Most of my money was spent traveling out here."

Alex watched as Daniel pulled her out the kitchen's back door and down the path toward the barn.

"Honey, we'll get you set up with some household money. Don't worry," Alex told her, thinking somehow he needed to make certain she had the funds she needed. Soon it would be winter and she would need all kinds of winter gear.

"Come on, we're almost there," Daniel told her as he led her into the barn.

"I smell horses," she said.

Neither one of them confirmed her suspicions.

Alex went to the stall and led the beautiful Appaloosa mare toward Francis. Daniel held up her hand to the horse's nose and she sniffed and then licked the back of her hand.

"Oh, is it a horse?" she said excitedly.

Daniel pulled the handkerchief from her eyes. "She's yours to ride about the ranch or into town."

Francis ran her hand down the horse's neck and flank. "She's beautiful. Thank you."

"You do know how to ride?" Alex asked.

"Of course," she said smiling. "I had to leave my horse behind in South Carolina."

Alex walked over to the wall where the saddles hung. He pulled down the one he wanted.

"We don't have a side saddle," he said.

She laughed. "Don't worry. I would never have used one. Talk about a death trap. With a jolt, you can go flying out of the saddle. No, I'll take my chances with a regular saddle."

Quickly, Alex began to saddle the horse while Daniel moved to their horses and prepared them for their ride.

"Are we going riding?" Francis asked.

"Yes, I thought you might like to see the ranch," Alex said.

"Oh my, yes," she replied.

As soon as the horse was ready, she stepped up into the stirrup and sank down on the saddle. Leaning over, she rubbed the horse's crest and then worked her way down his neck and even his throat.

"You're such a beautiful girl," she said, talking to the mare.

When Daniel finished saddling their horses, Alex stepped into his stirrup and rode out of the barn. Francis followed him with Daniel last.

For the next hour, they rode the main area of the ranch showing her the land and telling her their plans.

Alex could see she was a good horsewoman and knew how to ride very well. There were no worries, and most of the horses, if you turned them loose, would return to the barn. They knew where their feed and water were.

Finally, they came to his favorite part of the ranch where they had picnicked once before.

Daniel helped her down from the horse and she reached up and gently kissed him on the lips.

"It's been too long," she said with a grin.

Then she grabbed the picnic basket and went to the big pine tree. She spread the blanket and began to fix their plates.

There was only one way he would enjoy this picnic better.

"Take off your dress," Alex told her as he sank down on the blanket.

She glanced at him. "I want us to talk after lunch."

"And we will," Daniel told her. "But first remove your dress. If you don't do it, you'll receive a spanking."

Shaking her head, she lifted the dress over her head.

"See I'm not wearing anything beneath it."

"No, but damn, I love to look at your breasts."

"And those sweet pussy lips," Daniel said, sinking down on the blanket beside her.

She handed him a plate of fried chicken and potato salad that the cook had sent home with them last night.

"Eat up men, you're going to need your strength," she said and handed Alex a plate.

He took it from her, and for the next several minutes, they ate their meal.

"Tell me about your families," she said.

"Not much to tell," Alex told her. "They're all dead."

"Oh my, I'm so, so sorry," she said.

He shrugged his shoulders. "They were killed in a fire deliberately set by Daniel's uncle."

"What?" she said, her sapphire eyes large. "Why would he do that?"

"My father refused to pay the protection money Daniel's uncle insisted on. My father had a small store in Kansas City, Missouri. To keep him from being robbed, Daniel's uncle started requiring everyone to pay him money. But my father was as stubborn as they come and he refused."

Shaking her head, she gazed at Daniel her eyes questioning.

"My family is a notorious outlaw family. My real name is

not Smith," Daniel said. "Alex was searching for my uncle. It's how we met. It's how we became bounty hunters. Because I helped him locate my uncle and together we collected the money."

She licked her lips. "You were bounty hunters?"

"Yes, that's how we made our money," Alex said. "But we gave it up after we made enough to buy the land. We were tired of thieves shooting at us."

Alex watched as she swallowed hard.

"Bounty hunters," she said.

"Is that a problem?" Daniel asked.

"Oh no, it's just that is such a dangerous profession. You could have been hurt or killed."

Daniel leaned back on his elbow and stared at her. "That's why we no longer do it."

Alex noticed that her hands were shaking.

"Who is your outlaw family?"

Daniel did not like to tell people his real last name, because if someone let it slip, they could find him.

"They're from Missouri, but I don't tell anyone, because I don't want them locating me," he said, gazing at her with an odd expression.

"Darling, tell us about your family," Alex said, wondering if she were hiding something about her family.

Francis took a deep breath. "It was just me and my sister and my mother who has slowly been losing her mind since my father died. There was no chance of me finding a good husband and so instead of me eating up food in the house, I left for Charleston."

"What did your sister do?" Alex asked, trying to see what had made her so nervous.

"She is going to marry the lawyer in town," she said. "Hopefully, he will take care of her and Momma."

There was something off and Alex could not put his hands on what was wrong. But then again, he just wanted to put his hands on Francis.

"I bet it was hard to leave them behind knowing you would never see them again," Daniel said, gazing at her.

Tears welled in her eyes. "Yes, I miss them so much."

"Next time we go into town, you can send a letter to them," Alex said.

Her eyes widened and she licked her lips. "Yes, that's a good idea."

Why did he get the feeling she was just saying what she knew he wanted to hear? Something was wrong, but he didn't know what.

Alex moved to the picnic basket and threw their dishes inside. Then he pulled out a bottle of honey.

"Oh my, look what I found here," he said.

Daniel started to laugh. "I put the bottle in the picnic basket at the last moment."

He crawled over to Francis and pushed her back on the blanket. Then he opened the bottle of honey and poured some on her breasts.

Francis gasped. "What are you doing?"

"I'm going to eat my honey," he said and then he poured some between the vee of her legs.

Daniel watched Alex before he moved to Francis's side. He

unbuttoned his pants and his hard cock sprang free. He took the jar of honey and poured some on his penis.

"Darling, I've got something for you," Daniel said as he pushed his cock into her mouth just as Alex moved down between her legs.

Suddenly Francis gasped as Alex's tongue lapped up the honey between her legs. His fingers worked over her clit as his tongue dove inside.

She moaned loudly.

"Do that again, Alex. She's moaning all over my cock," he said.

Alex spread the lips of her pussy and she widened her legs. He paid particular attention to her clit, causing her hips to rise off the ground as he lapped at the nectar.

"That's it, baby, suck my cock," Daniel said. "Oh, God, you are getting so good at this. I'm going to come and when I do, you swallow it all."

Alex reached down and grabbed the butt plug in her ass and twisted the dowel.

She screamed around Daniel's cock and the man grabbed her head and held her tightly against him as he came in her mouth.

Then he pushed away from her.

"Darling, that was so good," he told her.

"Alex," she moaned. "Can I come?"

"Not yet," he told her. He wanted to test her ability to restrain herself from coming. He nipped at her clit and then he eased up, unbuttoned his fly, and pulled out his rock-hard cock.

"I need to be inside you," he told her. "I need to feel you squeezing me."

"Alex," she moaned.

He slapped her on her pussy and she drew up her legs. She was fighting it so hard. He could tell the least little thing and she would be over the edge.

Gripping her legs, he spread her wide and slammed his cock home.

"Oh," she cried. "Oh, Alex."

He halted and she tried to move her hips to get him going.

"What do you want?"

"Please, Alex, I need you," she said.

"What is it you need?"

"I need your cock. Please give me your cock."

He smiled. "With pleasure."

Lifting her hips, he rammed into her again and again, each time more forceful than the last.

She bit her lip, trying to hold back the orgasm, and closed her eyes.

"Open your eyes and look at me. I want you looking at me when you come."

"Can I come?"

"Yes," he said as he pummeled her one last time before his seed exploded from his cock coating her pussy.

He collapsed on top of her, feeling her breasts crushed against his chest, his breathing labored as his body slowly came down. She gazed at him and then she reached up and kissed him.

It was a kiss of a satisfied woman as she clung to him.

When they finally separated, she gazed at him. "Thank you. Both of you have made my life so wonderful. I'm so glad I took a chance and came to Treasure Falls."

But why did he get the feeling there was more to her story than her just hopping on a stage and coming to Montana? What was their bride hiding?

CHAPTER 15

The next morning Daniel and Alex rode out to check on the herd and make certain they still had hay. Francis stood naked at the door waving good-bye to them. She blew them a kiss.

"Hurry home," she said with a smile.

Damn, that was hard to ride away from. She promised to have their dinner ready when they came home and Daniel could hardly wait.

Their wedding was over, and though Daniel loved every moment of the last few days, he also was nervous. He'd been a bounty hunter for many years, he'd lived with a criminal family, and he knew the signs when someone wasn't being honest.

Francis had not told them everything about her past. There was something she was hiding and he didn't know what. And that disturbed him.

Alex sat in his saddle, swaying with the rhythm of his horse.

"The last two days have been mighty fun," Daniel said. "I'm glad you talked me into marriage."

"Yes, and I notice you haven't been pulling out like you said you were going to. So you must have stopped worrying about producing a demon child."

A flock of birds flew up in front of them.

"Nope, I'm still worried, but when you're in the moment, it's awfully hard to pull out. When it feels so good, you don't think about what could happen."

His friend chuckled. "I'm not even going to try. I'm really enjoying being with Francis. I like the fact that she's open to trying new things."

Last night, they had tied her to the bed and taken advantage of her every way possible, except for anal sex. She wasn't ready. Though she was on her second butt plug.

"Do you get the feeling she's not telling us everything about why she left South Carolina?"

Alex whirled around to glance at Daniel. "Yes. Did you see the way her hands were trembling yesterday when she learned we were former bounty hunters? She looked scared."

The expression on her face and the way her hands trembled were signs that something wasn't right. Why was she afraid of them being bounty hunters?

"I did," Daniel said, wondering what would cause her to act so frightened. "You don't think she's gotten into trouble with the law?"

"Not our sweet girl," Alex said. "But I wonder if her sister or maybe even her father? Maybe he's not dead and she's afraid we'll go after him."

There was silence as they each contemplated what she could be hiding. Why was their sweet wife afraid of their previous profession? For the next mile, they rode in silence, but just before they came up on the herd, Daniel knew he had to ask the question.

"You remember how when we first met her, she had a broken wrist?"

"Yes," Alex said. "What has that got to do with anything?"

"Don't know," Daniel said. "Right now, it's all a big puzzle."

They rode along, swaying in their saddles, the mountains in the background. Soon their tops would be covered with snow.

"Do you think we should talk to her about it tonight?"

"Maybe we mention that there should be no secrets between us," Alex said. "Or maybe one of us should ride into town and speak to the sheriff. Maybe even take a look at the wanted posters to see if there is anyone wanted by the last name of Little."

They each sighed.

"What would we do if one of her family members is wanted?"

"Nothing. But I would rather she told us than for us to learn the truth. Maybe we should give her a chance to tell us tonight. Then if we don't learn anything, I'll go into town tomorrow and see what I can find out. We could be worrying for nothing."

Daniel nodded. "Let's ask her more direct questions

tonight and see what she says."

They stopped their horses at the top of the hill and gazed down at their herd.

"We're so damn lucky," Daniel said. "We could be back in Missouri stealing and going to jail."

"That was your life. Mine was destroyed by your uncle. No, I don't ever want to return to that hellhole. Look what we have here. Gorgeous mountains, pine trees, and valleys filled with grass to feed our cattle. We are very blessed. And soon we'll have little children running through the house."

Daniel shook his head. "I've got to remember to pull out. My seed is tainted and I'm risking everything just being married."

Alex shook his head. "Man, I wish you would get over this obsession. Look at the man you've become. Look at the man your children will look up and call Papa. Do you really think that after seeing you, they will become pawns of the devil?"

Daniel sighed. He'd thought so much about this. Yes, he wanted children, but he feared they would become like his family. And that could never be.

"What if you have girls?"

He gave a chuckle. "Do you really think the women in my family were sweet little grandmas that made cookies and gave hugs? Oh, hell no. My grandmother ran a boarding house and you best not be late on the rent. She also had a pig pen and pigs, they'll eat anything. I know at least two late on the rent troublemakers, as she called them, disappeared in the pig pen."

"Damn," Alex said. "That's cold."

"My aunt, she ran a whorehouse and she was the meanest

madam that I've ever known. You didn't cross her and you damn sure didn't hurt her girls. Of course, she was also known to take a strap to an unruly girl. Or give her the worst patrons."

Daniel's childhood had never been innocent or sweet. He accompanied his papa on his first raid when he was eight. It happened not long after his mother was killed. Murdered to be precise, but somehow they made it appear like an accident.

His sister had been taught how to cheat at cards, and to this day, she worked in a gambling house, cheating men out of their hard-earned dollars.

Last he heard, his two other brothers were riding with a gang, robbing banks.

The sheriff had raided his home at least twice while he was a child, but they had never found anything they were searching for because it was all hidden in an abandoned well.

"Your family is mean and vicious, but I still believe your children will not be living in that kind of environment and will not turn out like your brothers or even your father."

"Maybe," Daniel said. "But it also terrifies me that they might find me and steal what I love the most. My family, Francis, you and our children."

"That's not going to happen unless they're ready to die."

They rode down the hill toward the cattle, knowing it was time to get to work.

"So, tonight we'll speak to Francis about her hiding secrets."

"Yes," Daniel said, knowing full well she was keeping something from them, but not certain what.

CHAPTER 16

*H*ow in the hell had she become married to not one, but two bounty hunters? There was a price on her head and her husbands could turn her in and be rewarded with a sizable reward.

As they rode off, she gazed at them and thought of leaving. If she left, they could not turn her in, but where would she go?

Standing at the door, she knew she could not leave them. Already she was falling in love with each of them. They were good men. She had a good life here. She only hoped that the law didn't follow her here.

Turning from the door, she quickly tackled the breakfast dishes, getting them cleaned. Then she worked on what they would have for supper. Afterward, she cleaned the bedroom before she went down to make a cake.

Tonight, she would have their dinner ready when they returned. She'd have baths prepared for them both, and afterward, she would enjoy both of them. So far she loved being married and could only see happiness in front of her.

After she put the cake in the oven, she filled a pan with hot water to wash clothes. Her husbands had several pairs of pants that were dirty and there were so many shirts.

Carrying the hot water outside, she poured it into the wash tub and began to scrub the clothes.

The chickens clucked nearby, scratching the dirt looking for feed.

As she finished rinsing the clothes, she noticed the birds had gone silent. A rustle in the woods had her glancing up.

"Who's there?" she called.

More silence. An eerie feeling slid down her spine. She was naked. If anyone rode up, they would see how vulnerable she appeared.

The whinny of a horse confirmed her worst fears. She dashed into the house and locked the door behind her. Then she ran to the front door and closed and bolted it shut. Glancing outside, she strained to see who might have seen her.

If it was a neighbor, didn't they know not to visit them the first week? Alex promised her that everyone knew better than to visit the newlyweds.

What if it was the law? What if they had found her? How could she continue to live this way, always in fear? Maybe she should just turn herself in and that way her husbands could move on with their lives without her.

Then she saw a man moving about outside. She didn't

recognize him. His gun was drawn and fear spiraled through her as he moved in a stealthy manner toward the house.

She searched for a weapon. Anything to protect herself and realized she was still naked. But there was nothing she could do about it now.

She remembered the shotgun near the front door. Quickly she grabbed it and made sure it was loaded and ready to fire.

Suddenly, the glass window shattered and she knew the man was intent on getting into the house.

Peering out the window, she saw him, raised the shotgun, and fired at him from the broken window.

"Son of a bitch," the man said. "Daniel, get out here now. I know you're in there. We need to talk."

"Who are you?" Francis called. "Daniel's not here."

She hated admitting that, but she was not afraid to fight the man off.

"I know he lives here. You tell him his cousin Frank needs to speak to him. I'll be in town tomorrow morning at the cafe. Tell him to meet me there at ten in the morning or I'll come back and burn this place to the ground."

Francis lifted the gun and shot at him again. "And I'll fill your backside with buckshot."

"Who are you?"

"I'm his wife and I don't appreciate your threats. Now get the hell off of our property," she said and fired the gun again.

"You're a mean little spitfire. You tell him Frank was here," the man said and hurried off into the bushes.

Why would his cousin try to break in? Why would he be here now? Daniel admitted he came from a family of outlaws.

But he had told her that no one knew where he lived. So why was this man showing up now?

Later that afternoon, the men came riding back in. As soon as they came to the house, they rattled the door.

"Francis, why's the door locked?"

She ran to the door and let them in.

"Because your cousin Frank tried to break in this afternoon," she said.

Daniel came around and took her in his arms. It was then that he noticed the broken window. She had cleaned up the glass, but the windowpane was gone.

"What happened?"

"He broke the glass and tried to come in. I used the shotgun on him," she said. "It kept him from getting any closer."

Stunned, the two men stared at her. "Are you all right?"

"I'm fine. My gun sent him on his way," she said, stepping out of Daniel's arms and going to the stove. She pulled out the roast and set it on the table. Her cake was sitting on the counter.

"Wow, a cake," Alex said.

"Wait a minute," Daniel said. "How do you know it was my cousin."

"Because he told me so," she said. "And when he threatened to set the place on fire, I aimed the shotgun at him and showered him with buckshot. He better not be making any more threats, or I'll do it again."

She sat a fresh bowl of corn on the table. "Wash up. It's time to eat."

"What else did he say," Daniel asked, stepping closer to her.

"Oh, he mentioned that he wants you to meet him at the cafe tomorrow morning at ten. He needs to speak to you. But why in the world would he try to break in and frighten me to get you to meet with him in person?"

Her two men turned and stared at one another. There was something that they had not told her.

"Is this cousin from your outlaw family that you didn't want to know where you lived?"

Daniel's face turned to stone and she could see the anger resonating from his eyes.

"Yes," he said softly.

Taking her by the hand, he led her into the living room and sat her on the couch. "My real name is Daniel James. My family lives in Missouri and was very involved in the Civil War. They're all criminals. I grew up in a family of criminals. I went on my first raid when I was eight."

Astounded, Francis stared at him. "Is Jesse James your cousin?"

"Yes," he said. "The family is notorious for their criminal dealings."

For a moment, she stared at Daniel. Her husband was a member of a family that robbed banks, stole personal belongings, and murdered many Union soldiers. And yet it wasn't his fault.

"What is your cousin doing here? I didn't think you wanted the family to know where you lived," she said.

"I didn't. This is the first time they've found me," he said with a sigh. "Tomorrow, Alex will stay here with you while I go into town and meet him."

"No, you won't," both she and Alex said at the same time.

"I know how to protect myself. Believe me, I know how to use a gun. But you need Alex with you. I don't want you going alone," she said.

Alex nodded. "Agree. We'll meet your cousin tomorrow and do some other business we need to take care of and then we'll get home as soon as possible. You will keep the windows and doors locked. Don't open up for anyone."

"Yes," she said, fearing for these two men she was falling in love with. "But, tonight, we're going to eat dinner. I have water heating on the stove for both of you to bathe in. And then I'll guess we'll call it a night and go to sleep."

Alex laughed. "After we give our wife a thorough fucking."

"Yes," Daniel said as the two men surrounded her. "It's what I've thought about all day long."

She reached up and kissed Daniel hard on the mouth, her lips taking control. Abruptly, she ended the kiss and turned to Alex.

Staring up into his emerald eyes, she grinned mischievously. "You're going to fuck me tonight?"

"Yes, darling," he said. "And if you don't stop teasing me, it will be after dinner. It might be right here on the table with you as the centerpiece."

She laughed. "Then we better eat."

CHAPTER 17

*D*aniel was furious as they rode into town. "How the hell did he find us?"

"Don't know," Alex said. "We covered our tracks very well."

"I know," Daniel said, wondering if it was just Frank who knew his location. Or did the others as well. And if they ever learned about their ranch, they would all be coming this way. They were leeches.

"We didn't talk to Francis last night about our suspicions," Alex said.

"No, just hearing how Frank had tried to break in frightened me. Are you certain you shouldn't turn around and go back?"

Alex laughed. "The woman knows how to protect herself. But I did tell her that she had our permission to wear a dress today. She was naked yesterday when he tried to break in."

If Frank had done anything to harm or hurt Francis, the man would be dead today. As it was, he feared he could not control his rage when he spoke to the man. What the hell did he want?

As they rode into town, his nerves grew even tighter. He hated his family. It was the reason he'd moved without them knowing.

When they reached the cafe, he slid off his horse and tied the reins to the hitching post.

"Don't let him goad you into doing something stupid," Alex said as they walked up the wooden sidewalk. He entered the cafe and saw Frank sitting alone at a table.

He walked toward his cousin. It wasn't often that he wore his sidearms, but today, he had them on. With a click, he undid the snap that held the gun in the pocket. This way he could reach it quickly if needed.

When he reached the table, he stared at the man he never wanted to see again.

"What are you doing here, Frank?"

"Oh, it's my long-lost cousin. I should ask you the same thing. What in the hell are you doing in Montana, Daniel?" he asked. "Sit down. We've got lots to discuss."

Alex and Daniel pulled out chairs and sank down on them.

"Do you want some breakfast? This place has great food," he said.

"No," Daniel said and Alex shook his head.

"I see you're still hanging out with this loser," Frank said, nodding his head at Alex.

"What do you want?"

There were very few people in the café. The waitress, Sue,

who had been there as long as Alex and Daniel lived here, came over.

"You need a menu?"

"No, just a cup of coffee," Daniel said.

"Same," Alex replied.

"How did you find me?" Daniel asked.

His cousin looked so much like him and that was always a problem. He had the same dark hair and brown eyes and was built about the same height.

"Well, I wasn't looking for you, but I just happened to be following a trail of a woman who liked to rob banks. You see, I took a lesson from you and I've been doing some bounty hunting. I needed to get out of Missouri for a while and it seemed like a good way to make a living."

If the man had left the family behind, there was a reason. Since he was doing bounty hunting, he couldn't be wanted. Or at least Daniel didn't think so.

"What did you do that caused you to leave Missouri?"

The man laughed. "Well, my cock got me into trouble. The fifteen-year-old girl came up pregnant and her papa threatened to shoot me on sight if he found me. So I decided it was time to leave town for a while."

Disgust filled Daniel. Who in the hell would do that to a young woman? Were all the men in this family disgusting males who couldn't keep from trying to defile young women?

"So what brings you here?"

The man leaned back and gazed at him. "One of the mail-order brides that came out from Charleston is a wanted bank robber. Seems she liked to take the cash out of the Orangeburg bank. Plus, she shot a sheriff. Didn't kill him, but that was enough to make the bounty on her double. I aim to find that woman and take the cash."

A spiral of fear gripped Daniel. No, it couldn't be Francis.

"Her name is Francis and then I saw in the paper that Alexander Romney had married a Francis Little with Daniel Smith from Missouri standing as best man. As soon as I saw Alex's name, I knew it had to be you. What's the deal with the two husbands in this town? Do you share women?"

As far as Daniel was concerned, his cousin could wonder how a marriage with two husbands worked all he wanted because he was not about to inform him of the joys of two men taking a woman.

"So I'm wondering if this Francis Little could actually be Francis Nelson, the girl wanted for bank robbery and wounding a sheriff. Who last I heard was hot on her trail. In fact, he should be here just about any day."

Daniel stared at his cousin not willing to let him see his fear. "My wife is not Francis Nelson. She came from Charleston, not Orangeburg. And this sweet woman would never have the courage to pull off robbing a bank. You need to keep looking."

The man stared at him. "Yes, I was out there trying to get a good look at her yesterday when she started shooting at me. She seems to know how to handle a gun real well."

Alex who had been quiet suddenly spoke up. "That's because she has to know as a rancher's wife how to protect herself from vagrants and thieves and wild animals that like to come up when we're out working."

Frank smiled. "She was not friendly. I mean all I wanted to do was talk."

"And that's why you shot out our kitchen window?"

He shrugged. "I was trying to draw you out of the house, but you weren't there."

Daniel didn't believe him for one minute. He hoped to break in and take Francis. They would never have found her if he had managed to get to her. Thank goodness, they had left a fully loaded shotgun by the door.

"Francis is not your woman," Alex said.

"How do you know?" Frank asked.

"Because she's not a bank robber. And why would she shoot a sheriff?"

Daniel stood. He'd heard just about enough. "I think you need to continue on down the road. And don't even think about sending the family here. They'll get nothing from me but a bullet. Do you understand?"

A smile crossed Frank's face. "I'm not giving up until I know for certain that your Francis is not the person I'm searching for."

"Come near the house again and there will be a bullet with your name on it," Daniel told him.

Alex stood and together the two men walked out of the cafe.

"I think we've got trouble," Alex said once they were outside.

"I think you're right. Let's go see the sheriff and learn what he can tell us," Daniel said.

After climbing onto their horses, they rode down the street to the sheriff's office where they tied the reins to the hitching post, and then they walked up the sidewalk and entered his office.

"Alex and Daniel. What are you guys doing? Aren't you supposed to be on your honeymoon? Or are you guys already tired of being married?"

"Neither," Alex said with a grin.

"We have a question for you, Sheriff," Daniel said. "Do you have any wanted posters on a Francis Nelson?"

The law officer frowned. "We get so few women. Most of them are men. Let me look through this pile of new ones I just received. They came in on the last stage."

The man started to flip through the posters.

"Oh, here you go," he said frowning. "Hey, isn't she your bride?"

"Shit," Alex said, glancing at the likeness of Francis.

Daniel shook his head. "No, our wife could not have done this. This has to be a mistake."

The sheriff frowned. "You know, boys, I should go out and arrest her."

The two men glanced at him.

Alex sighed. "Would you give us some time? We need to find out her side and then we'll do whatever you want. If that means turning her in, then that's what we'll do."

"You won't run off with her, will you?"

"No, sir, that would just put a reward on our head and we love our ranch here," Daniel said. "I've made a vow to obey the law and I aim to continue."

"All right, boys, I'll give you three days to figure out what you're going to do, then I'm going to come arrest her," he said.

"Thanks," Alex told the man.

"Don't let her get away," he said.

"Can I have that poster," Alex asked. "I'd like to show her what we found."

The man smiled. "Just bring it back when you bring her in."

"Will do," Alex said.

"Oh, and by the way, there is a bounty hunter in the cafe that is wanted back in Missouri," Daniel said. "He's armed and dangerous. He's part of the James family out of Missouri."

"Shit," the lawman said. "I'll go over there right now and tell him to get out of town."

"Good idea," Daniel said as they walked out of the office.

CHAPTER 18

*A*ll day, Francis had been nervous as a newborn filly, watching the windows to see if her husbands had returned. She'd been waiting to learn what they found out about Daniel's cousin.

What was the man doing here? How had he found Daniel?

Finally, late in the afternoon, she heard their horses ride in. Dinner was almost ready and she couldn't wait to hear what the man said.

She opened the back door to the kitchen and stood there waiting, nude. All day, she had worn her dress, but when she knew it was her men, she'd tossed the garment.

It took them a few minutes to unsaddle their horses and then she saw them strolling toward the house.

They didn't appear happy. In fact, they looked angry.

Alex appeared to be holding a piece of paper in his hands.

"Alex, Daniel," she cried when they reached the door. "I'm so glad you're home."

They were silent. Something was wrong. Terribly wrong.

"Did you meet with your cousin?"

"Yes," Daniel said.

"Why is he here? How did he find you?"

"He's searching for you," he said his eyes cold.

"Me?"

A trickle of fear wound its way into her stomach and she felt sick. Was her past catching up to her?

"Yes, you," Alex said and held up the wanted poster.

Terror ripped through her and she knew she was in so much trouble.

"Did you rob the Orangeburg bank?"

With a sigh, she turned and walked into the living room where she plopped down on the horsehair couch. No more lying. Time for her to tell them everything. Time for her to confess.

They followed her into the living room and sat on either side of her.

"Tell us the truth," Alex said. "We've bought you three days, but that's all."

Three days before they would haul her before a jury and hang her.

"My father died not long after the Civil War. He was gunned down by a gang of Rebel soldiers who were going after anyone who fought for the Union. Papa died from his injuries and that left the three of us to run the farm. And we tried. Lord, how my sister and I tried to make enough money."

Her hands twisted together and a twinge from her wrist

reminded her of how hard she'd fought for everything, only to now lose her happiness.

"The taxes on our small farm were outrageous. We barely had enough food to eat and they were about to take the farm from us for unpaid taxes. I couldn't get a job at the saloon unless I wanted to be a whore, so I decided to rob the bank. It was my only recourse. My sister was trying to find a man to marry her, but that was taking too long. We were desperate."

The memory of her agonizing over what to do overwhelmed her and she felt the tears gather in her eyes.

"Without my sister or my mother knowing, I took some of my father's clothes and dressed like a man. Then I rode our fastest horse into town and there I robbed the bank. The first time it was so easy. I paid off the taxes on the house and even bought us some supplies."

Alex and Daniel exchanged a look.

"Did you do it again?" Daniel asked.

"Yes, I went back two more times. The second time, it was just as easy as the first. With that money, I bought seed for the farm and even paid our help when the cotton crop came in. But the third time, they were waiting for me."

She remembered how surprised she'd been when she ran out of the bank and saw the riders in the street. Though she'd ridden as fast as she could, they had followed her.

"This time, they came to the house. So they knew it was me. How they figured out, I don't know. But they came to the house and tied up my mother. She's fifty-eight years old. She doesn't remember from one day to the next. After they left, that's when my sister told me I had to leave. She gave me a flyer she had picked up about Treasure Falls Montana Brides."

Shaking her head, she knew she had to tell them everything.

"That night I said my good-byes, snuck out of the house, and rode a horse in the darkness toward Charleston. Only problem was that the sheriff followed me. I didn't know. It was dark and I didn't hear anything. When exhaustion overcame me, I stopped for the night. I had just started to fall asleep when he snuck into my camp and crawled on top of me."

Tears streamed down her face. "He said he was going to give me the best eight inches I'd ever had and then he tried to kiss me. I bit him. I pulled out my gun and shot him in the chest just below his shoulder. He grabbed my wrist, the one holding my gun, and twisted it until it snapped. With my other hand, I grabbed a log by my pallet and hit him over the head with it. I didn't want to kill him. But he was going to do horrible things to me against my will."

"Is that why you had a cast on your wrist?" Daniel asked.

"Yes, the marriage broker had the doctor look at it," she said, thinking she would forever be grateful to Mrs. Newton.

Alex's eyes darkened and his face turned red. Daniel sat quiet and tense and appeared ready to explode.

"I pushed his body off mine and then I made it appear like he was sleeping and rode on to Charleston. I'm so sorry I've dragged you into this. I never meant to be a bank robber or kill the sheriff. Honestly, I just wanted to take care of my family. I could not let them go hungry."

The two men glanced at one another.

"What you did was wrong," Alex said. "The law knows where you are. The good news is that you didn't kill the sheriff. He was only badly wounded."

She gave a little laugh. "I'm not so certain that's good news. Because when you send me back there, he will take advantage of me. I know it."

The two men glanced at one another.

"Why is your cousin searching for me?"

"Because he's become a bounty hunter, following in my footsteps."

"Oh no," she said.

"When he saw in the paper Alex's name and I was best man, he knew that he'd found me."

"But your family. You didn't want them to find you," she said.

"Yes," Daniel said.

Only the ticking of the clock could be heard in the room as they sat there.

"I'm sorry," she said. "I wanted to tell you, but I have been so happy here with the two of you. Truly, these are some of the best days of my life. I'll treasure them always. I'll go pack my bags and you can take me to the sheriff."

"Not yet," Alex said. "He's given us three days to come up with a plan on how to save you or we turn you in. But first, you weren't honest with us. You're going to be punished tonight."

Francis knew that meant she was going to be spanked, and while she understood their reasoning, she also knew she would not resist them. These were her last days with her husbands and she needed to be with them every moment she could before the law sent her back to South Carolina.

"Go upstairs and get into position," Daniel told her. "We'll be up in a few moments."

With a sigh, she stood and hurried up the stairs. Oh, how she loved this house, their bedroom, everything, and now because of her wanting to help her family, she would lose everything.

When she reached their bedroom, she crawled onto the bed and got into the position she knew they would want her in. Right now, she would do anything to make them happy. Anything, because in three days, she would be gone.

And then her life would be a living hell until the day she hung.

She had been wrong to rob the bank, but she would do anything to help the people she loved. Even committing a crime.

She heard her men come into the room and heard their clothes hit the floor. Daniel would pick his up and lay them on the chair. Alex would leave his for her to find. But she didn't care.

"Do you agree that you deserve to be punished," Alex asked her.

"Because I was not honest with you, I deserve to be punished. But just know that I will always protect those I love. If we were to have children, I would do whatever it took, even commit a crime, to protect our babies."

They were silent and then she felt Alex's hands rubbing her buttocks.

"You're right, Francis. You are being punished because you kept secrets from us," Daniel said.

Suddenly she felt a swish of air as a smack landed on her cheeks.

"Count," Alex said.

"One," she cried, knowing that this was not going to be a light punishment, but rather the hardest they had ever spanked her.

Smack.

"Two," she cried out, her voice rising.

Smack.

"Three," she said with a gasp as her buttocks began to burn. She had no idea how many he intended to give her, but they would not be easy.

Smack.

"Four," she said, tears gathering in the corners of her eyes.

Smack.

"Five," she screamed, not knowing how much more she could take. These were not the sexual arousal spankings but rather hard ones that hurt.

Smack.

"Six," she cried, tears rolling down her cheeks. "Please, Alex."

Smack.

"Seven," she sobbed. "I promise I will never keep secrets from you again."

Alex massaged her cheeks and it was both torturous and

exquisite. "If you had been honest, there would be no need to make your punishment hurt."

He moved her into his arms. "To make this work, we all have to be honest with no secrets between us. You know my secrets. How my family was killed by Daniel's uncle. I hate the James family and everything they do. But Daniel helped me locate him, and for that, I am forever grateful."

She wrapped her arms around his neck needing to feel the strength of his body. "You would do anything to protect those you love, just like me."

"Yes," Alex said quietly. "That's why we need to figure out how to keep you from being returned."

"I'm so sorry," she said. "I should have told you sooner."

Daniel wrapped his arms around Francis. "We'll figure something out."

Her two strong men's chests encircling her felt like she was encased in armor. Like nothing could harm her here.

But she knew her men were honorable and would do whatever the sheriff of Treasure Falls required.

Her bottom was burning, her emotions were all over the place, and she felt humiliated by what she had done and the spanking she'd received.

Alex slipped his fingers between her legs and pulled them out. "You're wet. You didn't like being punished, but you did like the spanking."

What could she say? She did like a spanking when they had done it while they were having sex, but today, Alex had shown her he was serious when it came to being open and honest. And she believed him.

He reached out and wiped her tears from her face. "Be honest with us, Francis, and you won't have to experience this kind of punishment again."

"I'm trying," she said.

Daniel moved behind her. His fingers teased her clit causing her to tighten around his digits as they moved over the lips. She moaned.

He thrust his fingers up into her pussy and she moaned knowing that soon, they would have her screaming with passion. His hands spread her cheeks and he put his mouth against her pussy and she groaned.

"Oh, that feels good," she said.

Bending behind her, Daniel's hands gripped her hips as he lifted her to where his mouth reached her center. He let his tongue work magic on her clit, her pussy lips, and even swirled that sweet instrument inside her. She groaned as heat spread through her.

Standing, he moved into position and slammed his cock into her pussy and she groaned at the feel of him stretching her, filling her, as she moved her hips to accommodate him. For a moment, they moved in unison as he held her hips, rocking her exactly like he wanted.

Alex reached for her nipples and twisted them. "Soon you're going to take our cocks. Both of them at the same time."

His mouth covered hers as a spiral of heat shot through her as Alex all but chewed her lip.

Between the two of them, they were sending her spiraling toward the edge.

She released Alex's mouth. "I'm going to come."

"Not yet, you're not," Daniel said and he slapped her ass, but this time between the two of them, it was more pleasure than pain.

"Daniel," she cried as she bit her lip to keep from coming.

When he twisted her clit with his fingers, she felt him tense and knew he was close.

"Now, you can come," he said as he slammed his cock against her womb, his seed spilling against the walls.

She screamed with pleasure, her body shaking and undulating as the orgasm rocked her over and over, plunging her headfirst over a cliff to land safely in her husband's arms.

Daniel and Francis collapsed on the bed. The two men moved her until she was between them.

"This is where you belong," Alex said as she slowly recovered. "This is how we will always protect you."

They lay there in silence as they tried to catch their breath.

"But how can you save me from the law?" she asked. "What I did was wrong, but it was for my loved ones."

"We'll find some way out of this mess," Daniel said. "Some way."

CHAPTER 19

The next morning, Alex woke them at dawn.

"Get up. I have an idea," he said. "We need to go talk to the sheriff. Francis, you have to tell the sheriff what you told me and Daniel."

Daniel and Francis hurried and got ready. Instead of taking the wagon, they all rode in on their horses. Francis wore a pair of bloomers for riding a horse that didn't show her legs. It was the only time they would allow her to wear bloomers.

When they arrived in town, it was still early, but they pulled up in front of the sheriff.

"Good morning," he said, standing outside his office. "You men are here awfully early. Are you bringing me Mrs. Romney?"

"No, Sheriff. I have an idea," Alex said. "We want to talk to you about our plan."

The men descended from their horses and Alex helped Francis alight.

"Good morning, Sheriff," she said as she walked inside.

The men followed her in and then they arranged chairs around the sheriff's desk.

"Ma'am, I have to ask you. Did you rob the bank?"

"Yes, Sheriff. The taxes were way overdue on the farm. They had doubled since the war and my papa was dead. We were starving and I couldn't find a respectable job. No, it wasn't right, but I did what I had to, to survive."

The man sighed and shook his head. "It's still against the law, ma'am. The depositors at the bank lost their money."

"I know, sir, and I'm sorry," she said. "But an empty belly makes poor decisions."

The sheriff chuckled. "So true."

"What if Daniel and I paid the bank back their money? Would that clear her?"

The sheriff frowned. "The bank would have to drop the charges. But I don't know why they wouldn't if you paid them back."

Daniel grinned. "We'll write them a nice letter and wire the money to them. We will also tell them that acceptance of this cash means that they will withdraw their charges."

That was a great idea. "Yes, by tying the acceptance of the cash to the charges, it puts the burden back on the bank. They are going to want to make their patrons happy and their depositors will just be glad to get the money back."

"That only leaves the charges the sheriff brought against her."

A sigh came from Francis. "Sheriff, do you remember when I arrived in town how I had a cast on my wrist?"

"Yes, ma'am," the sheriff said. "I was there when you stepped off that stage."

Francis closed her eyes for a moment and then she told the sheriff what happened that night. How the sheriff tried to give her *eight inches*. A blush spread across her beautiful cheeks when she told the man.

"If you let him take me, then I'm certain he will mistreat me right up until the day I hang," she said. "And believe me, this sheriff is not going to let me get away without hanging. A woman shot him in the shoulder. I've injured his pride. He won't drop the charges and he will insist on returning me to South Carolina."

The sheriff sighed. "I detest bad lawmen. They give all of us a bad name. And from the sounds of it, you're right. His pride is involved and he will refuse to drop the charges."

"Plus, we have a bounty hunter here searching for her," Daniel said. "My cousin."

The sheriff laughed. "I ran him out of town. Told him I wanted no part of the James gang here in our little place."

Alex knew the family, and you could tell them to leave, but that didn't mean they were gone. Even now, he was probably out at their house watching to see if he could catch Francis alone. They would have to be on constant guard.

"I tell you what. You had a good reason to shoot that sheriff. If Alex and Daniel will return the money to the bank and get them to drop the charges, then as far as I'm concerned, you're clear. But if that lawman shows up here, which I hate to say it, but if he's as stubborn as he sounds, he will, then we'll have to revisit this and see if we can get him to drop the charges. If he won't, you'll have to return to South Carolina."

Daniel and Alex glanced at one another. Honestly, it was the best they could do.

"Thank you, Sheriff," Francis said. "I fear you're right."

"Sheriff, I give you my word that we'll contact the bank and see about paying them back. If they refuse, we'll have no choice but to bring Francis in."

The men stood and shook hands with the sheriff.

Francis stood and reached over and kissed the man on the cheek. "Thank you for helping me. I do appreciate it."

"Yes, ma'am," the man said, grinning. "Now go enjoy your honeymoon."

When they walked out of the office, they turned toward the bank.

It didn't take them long to find out about wiring the money.

"Let's go home and we'll draft the letter to the bank," Alex said.

"No, let's go to Aunt Grace and get paper and do it there. Then we can mail it before we ride back home. This will save us a trip. I'm feeling nervous about being in town too much and I don't want to be left alone at the ranch. Not until this is settled."

The two men glanced at one another and smiled. "Good idea."

When they reached the doctor's house, Aunt Grace greeted them with open arms.

"I'm so happy to see you. You look radiant. How do you like married life?"

"I love it," Francis said. "But we've run into some trouble from back home. Do you have an ink quill and some paper we could borrow?"

"Of course, come in," the older woman said. "The doctor is out on a house call. Besides, I wanted to talk to you, Francis. There was a lawman, a sheriff, here earlier looking for you. What's that about?"

Stunned, they all stared at one another.

"He's here," Francis gasped. "Oh my God, he's here."

CHAPTER 20

*D*aniel had that tingling feeling sitting at the base of his spine that he knew was warning him trouble lay ahead.

They waited to leave town until after dark. Even traveling to their home in the dark, he was nervous, his hand rested on his gun ready at a second's notice. They were silent on the ride back to the house, listening for the sounds of someone following them.

Before they left town, Alex had gone to speak to the sheriff again to warn him, and also he'd taken the letter to the stage for it to go out to the Orangeburg Bank.

Now they waited on the bank situation. But the sheriff, that was the one he feared. And he'd already made up his mind that he would go with Francis back to Orangeburg, if he had to.

There was no way, he would let that man take her and get his hands on her. She was their wife.

When they turned down the lane to the house, he saw the fire.

"The barn's on fire," Alex said, racing toward the burning structure.

"Watch out," Daniel called, but he wasn't going to leave Francis.

This was a trick the James gang often used to separate people and it worked almost every time. Frank was just showing his hand.

"Get in the house and lock the doors. Don't you open them until you know for certain it's us," he said as they pulled up in front of the house.

Jumping down off his horse, he helped Francis down and then he shoved her into the house. He waited until he heard the lock click.

She was safe for now.

Racing toward the barn, he found Alex, searching around the burning structure.

The animals had gotten out and that was a relief. Right now, they didn't have any little ones, but come spring, their stalls would be filled with calves.

Daniel's mind raced trying to think of the tricks that they had taught him as a young kid. Set the barn on fire and the people in the house would come running out to put it out and…

"He's in the house," Daniel cried. "Shit, I just put Francis in there."

He raced toward the house, pulling his gun out. He kicked in the back door and saw Frank through the front windows, shoving Francis up in front of him on his horse. Her hands were tied and she looked defeated.

They ran through the house and out the front door.

"Stop," Alex called.

Frank turned and fired his gun at Alex as he galloped down the road. Alex dove into a nearby shrub.

"Damn, I hate your family," Alex shouted.

"Me too. Come on, we can catch them," Daniel told him.

In the darkness, it was so dangerous to race a horse, but they were. Frank had Francis, and they had to reach her before he turned her in to collect the reward. They had to reach her before the sheriff found them.

Frank turned and fired at them and Daniel felt the bullet whiz by his ear. Son of a bitch would kill him to take something he wanted away.

They were gaining on him and Daniel had no idea of how they were going to get Francis away from him without one of them getting killed.

The flash of a gunshot lit up the night and the bullet zinged between Daniel and Alex.

"Slow down," Alex said. "He's headed toward the falls."

Daniel pulled his horse to a slow trot. "Why aren't we going to trap him?"

"We are. We just need to let him feel like he's lost us. Then we surround him."

Daniel wanted to go full speed ahead. He didn't like the idea of his cousin getting away with Francis. The James gang, including his own father, had raped so many women.

They were close enough you could hear the falls, which drowned out the horses' hooves. Would Frank be stupid enough to stop and camp tonight at the falls?

Surely the man wasn't that unwise.

CHAPTER 21

*F*rancis was terrified. She no longer heard her men chasing after her. All she could hear was the sound of the waterfalls.

"Where the hell is that turnoff?" the man said.

There was no way she was going to help him. Because if he didn't turn on the road to the falls, then they would soon be in town and hopefully she could get help. But where were her men?

"Seems like that last bullet hit Daniel and Alex," he chuckled. "No one is behind us anymore."

A bullet would not have stopped her men. She knew that. Unless they were dead. She prayed they were setting up a trap.

The man found the turnoff and they rode toward the falls. Sitting in front of him, she could smell his unwashed body, the smoke, and the liquor on his breath. He may be Daniel's cousin, but he was disgusting.

Frank James was not a good man and she had no doubts about her fate with him.

As they rode toward the water, a fire was burning next to the falls. Who was here?

"About damn time," a voice she recognized called out. "I was beginning to think you were dead."

Oh my God, no, not the sheriff. He'd followed her all the way from South Carolina.

"Do you have the money?" Frank asked.

"Yes," her nemesis said.

Frank pulled on the reins of his horse. The animal neighed. Suddenly he shoved her out of the saddle and she fell to the ground landing with a hard thud.

"That's the way a woman is supposed to be treated," the sheriff said with a laugh. He grabbed her arm before she could stand and pulled her to her feet. "This time you're not getting away."

"How's the shoulder, Sheriff?"

"Hurts like a son of a bitch," he said. "You'll pay for that."

"How's the wrist," he asked laughing. "I should have broken both of them."

"It's perfectly fine," she said, thinking he smelled no better than Frank.

"You thought you got away with robbing the bank and shooting me. But you were wrong. I've been on your trail since right after you left Charleston."

An owl hooted in the night and the sheriff dragged her closer to the fire.

"My money, Sheriff," Frank said. "I delivered. Now it's your turn."

"Just a minute. Let me tie her up, then I'll get you your cash," he said, grinning at her. "Nothing is going to stop me from giving you eight inches of the best cock you've ever experienced."

She wanted to spit in his face but that would only bring more misery on her. Hopefully, somewhere in these woods, her husbands were searching for her.

The sheriff wrapped a rough rope around her wrists, making the knot tight. "Don't go anywhere. I'll be right back. Then we'll have our little party."

He went to his saddle bags to get the money. Frank sat on his horse watching him. But from the angle of the horse and the firelight, he didn't see the rifle until it was too late.

Bam. The rifle went off, the sound ricocheting, bouncing off the walls of the falls and the mountain surrounding them.

The man fell off his horse and landed on the ground next to the pond.

"Good riddance," the sheriff said. "I wasn't going to pay him your reward money. Hell, he's part of that James gang and doesn't deserve it. He's probably wanted himself."

Terror seized Francis as she sat next to the fire, afraid she would be next.

"Heard you got married," the sheriff said. "This damn town is full of sinners. You married two men, not one? Damn, that's bigamy. Another crime against you. Girl, you are going to swing. And I'm going to enjoy watching you hang. But until then, we can have us some fun."

She knew he was trying to goad her and she refused to give him the satisfaction.

"Now we wait because I'm sure your two lovers are going to come searching for you. They're going to think they can rescue you from the big, bad sheriff."

He laughed and stood over her with the rifle in his hands.

Suddenly there were sparkly lights dancing on the water. In disbelief, she saw an Indian man and woman. They shimmered over the water and smiled at her. The woman blew her a kiss.

"Do you see that? What the hell?" the sheriff said, running to the water. "Get out of there. You're under arrest."

The Indian man laughed and then he shook his head and looked up at the waterfall.

The sheriff tried to reach out to them, but instead, he fell into the pond right below the falls. A huge boulder rolled down the hill and over the top of the waterfalls. The rock landed on him, killing him instantly.

Speechless, Francis sat by the fire with her hands tied. What had just happened?

The Indian woman blew her another kiss and the man waved before they disappeared. Had she just seen the legend of Treasure Falls? Were they the Indian couple who had run away together and died when they jumped from the falls?

Racing footsteps came toward her and she was almost afraid to see who was there. Alex came running out of the darkness.

"Did you see that?"

"Yes," she said. "Thank God, you're all right. I was so worried when you disappeared."

Daniel came running from the opposite direction. "I can't believe what I just saw. It's the legend. The Indian warrior and princess saved you. They killed the sheriff."

Francis held her wrists up. The rope was cutting off the circulation and she was beginning to hurt. "Please, cut this off me."

Alex reached into his pocket and pulled out a knife. Quickly he sliced through the ropes and then she fell into his arms. Daniel came up behind her and she loved the feel of her men holding her.

"Francis, I'm sorry. I never thought about him being in the house," Daniel said.

"No, it's not your fault. I'm just so glad it's over."

"And I heard what the sheriff said to you. It was all I could do not to kill him myself," Alex said. "You were right. He would have abused you until you hung."

"The sheriff is dead. Your cousin is dead, and hopefully I will be pardoned by the bank," she said. "Then we can live our lives without fearing what will happen tomorrow."

"Yes," Daniel said, kissing the side of her neck.

"Yes, please," Alex said.

"Now take me home and let me show you how much you mean to me," Francis said.

They loaded up the dead bodies on their horses, kicked the fire out, and then Francis rode in front of Daniel.

"Darling, I didn't want to get married, but damn, now that you're here, I can't let you go."

She smiled up at him. "I'm glad."

She reached up and ran her hand down his cheek. "Let's go home."

"Gladly," Daniel told her and they rode out away from Treasure Falls.

CHAPTER 22

Hen they arrived home, they sat on the couch. Silence filled the room and she curled up in Alex's lap, needing to be close to her husband. "When you stopped following us, I thought you'd been shot."

"No, darling, we were surrounding him. We were not going to let him get away from us. But it was quite a shocker to see the sheriff waiting for him."

"It was terrifying. I knew he would hurt me."

"Right now, I need to feel my wife's naked arms around me."

"Me too," Daniel said. "Since we learned about your past, it's been a weird couple of days. All I want to do is spend time in your arms with me deep inside you."

Francis couldn't wait to experience the joy she always found in her husbands' arms. Standing, she took each man by the hand. "Let's go to bed."

They walked into the bedroom and removed their clothes.

Slowly she began to unbutton her dress. She removed her petticoats and stood before them naked.

Alex walked over to the dresser where he selected a larger plug from the wooden box and a jar of ointment. "This is the last plug. I want to see you work this into your ass. Afterward, I'm going to spank you and you are not allowed to come."

She tilted her dark curls in one direction. "Why are you punishing me? I did everything I could to stop Frank and the sheriff."

"Agree," Alex said. "This time it's for pleasure."

She smiled and hurried to do his bidding.

"Tonight, once we think you're ready, we're going to claim you, together. Alex will take your pussy and me your ass," Daniel said, handing her the last plug. "Put it in."

Pursing her lips, she glanced between them and then took the plug. Daniel handed her the lube and watched as she greased up the end. She placed the object between her legs but paused.

"We've had a couple of trying days. But I want you to know, I like the fact that you're in control. I like what we do together. I like it when you spank me, but not when you're punishing me."

"Don't disobey and I won't spank you so hard," Alex said.

Francis smiled at Alex as she reached up and stroked his face.

"Put the plug in," Alex told her, placing a hand on her knee. She dropped her legs open wide and rubbed the dowel through her wet, glistening pussy. The anticipation of both of them claiming her had her pussy throbbing.

She wanted to experience both of them at the same time. She was ready.

Slowly, she inched the plug in, breathing deeply pushing and pulling, she bit her lip as the fake cock popped into place. For a moment, she simply breathed as her body adjusted to the new, larger size. There were no other plugs, this was the end, and tonight she would experience both of her husbands at the same time.

Now they could finally claim her as theirs and she couldn't wait.

"Good girl," Daniel said.

Daniel swatted her ass sending ripples up through the plug and her body. She gasped and turned her gaze on him.

"Over my knee," Daniel demanded as he sank down onto the bed.

Alex stood to the side and helped her up and over Daniel's lap before he began to stroke his long, hard cock. Rubbing the bead of come that spilled from the end, Francis watched, mesmerized.

Daniel leaned down and kissed her on the ass, running his tongue along the seam of her cheeks. "No one messes with our woman and you're ours. Do you understand?"

"Yes," she whispered. "I'm yours. Take me at the same time, so I can experience both of my men."

This was what she needed. What she wanted. Her two men to show her they cared.

Daniel raised his hand and connected his palm with her rounded cheeks.

Smack!

Alex gripped her breasts in his hands, massaging and twisting her nipples. There were explosions of desire coming from so many places on her body that she moaned.

"Daniel," she cried out, her hands searching for something to grip onto.

Smack.

He paddled her again and again in rapid succession. Then he would let his fingers linger near her clit or brush them against that little button.

Subtle differences that she realized were making her orgasm build within her.

A moan escaped deep from her throat.

To change the rhythm, he spanked her first rapidly and then slowly and methodically, taking care to make certain that her entire ass went from white to a blushing pink.

"Daniel," she moaned feeling so close to coming. Though she knew that Alex had spanked her harder, Daniel's was more sexual, sensuous, and left her breathing hard, lifting her ass to meet him.

Alex slid his fingers over her folds before he plunged them inside her. When he pulled them out, they could see the wetness. "She's dripping."

She turned and gazed at Daniel.

"Please, fuck me," she cried.

Picking her up, Alex laid her on the bed on her back. Immediately, she spread her legs wide.

"Do you want to come?"

A smile spread across her face. "Yes. I need both of you. I'm ready for you both to claim me. Make me yours."

"Yes," Daniel said. "And we can't wait to fuck you."

Her ass was warm and ached, but beneath the pain, pleasure rode her hard. Lying on the bed, she was anxious, and her body yearned for her men to fill her. Never in a million years had she dreamed that pleasure could come from pain, and she liked that her men took charge of her and were rough and domineering.

Never had she dreamed that two men would satisfy her in ways she never imagined. For days, she'd stretched and trained her ass. Even now, the largest plug resided deep inside her, waiting for her men to remove it. Waiting for them to claim her ass.

While she trembled with anticipation, she knew she couldn't wait to feel them deep inside her at the same time.

Daniel rubbed lube over his long hard cock.

Alex lay beside her and then pulled her on top of him. His emerald eyes gazed into hers. "Are you ready?"

"Yes," she whispered. "I want both of you at the same time."

A grin spread across his face.

On the bed, he lay back, his head on the pillows, his cock standing at attention. All for her, and her pussy clenched as she stared at his massive cock. She could hardly wait to be filled by him.

"Climb on top and put my cock in your pussy," Alex said with a groan.

Gladly, she lifted a leg over him and moved into position, her hands resting on his chest. Leaning on him, she realized the strength of Alex.

All man. Powerful and seductive. Her man. Her husband. Her true love.

The bed shifted and Daniel climbed behind her. His tongue caressed her cheeks. A groan escaped her and she pushed back, needing more of his tongue, but he pushed her toward Alex.

"Grip Alex's cock with your pussy when I bury my cock deep inside your ass."

A tremor of nerves skittered along her spine.

"Will it hurt?"

"No, honey, we're going to make you feel so good," Daniel said. "Just relax and let me in."

Rising above Alex, she slid down over his hard cock. At the feel of him, she leaned back as she went lower and lower until she hit his pelvis. The feel of his long, hard cock, snug in her pussy was almost enough to send her over the edge. The plug in her ass was tight against him.

All the pleasure from before returned, swamping her with lust. She gasped. Filled with cock and the plug, she was so full, so tight, and yet she wanted more.

She wanted Daniel.

She began to move up and down on Alex's rigid member, rubbing her clit, needing to ride the pleasure building inside her.

Daniel's hand caressed her buttocks, his hand rubbing her ass, pressing her more toward Alex. Her breasts rubbed against his chest creating even more sparks.

As she hovered over Alex's chest, her nipples brushed against his hair, rubbing and abrading them. He gripped her face and kissed her. A moan escaped her as their tongues tangled and still she wanted more.

She wanted both of her men. Inside her now.

Daniel pulled the plug from her ass with one hand while the other one fondled her clit. When the plug came free, she felt like she was opened wide, empty and bereft. A moan escaped her.

"Oh, Daniel, this is what we've been wanting. Fuck me."

Leaning over, she felt the flared head of Daniel's hard cock press against her trained ass. Pressing forward, her anal muscles resisted though she tried to relax. Slick and hot, the pressure of his invasion grew. Slowly he pushed his rock-hard cock into her, her muscles quivered with submission as he filled her, stretching her.

"Relax, honey. It will be easier if you relax," Daniel told her.

The feel of both of them in her body was tight. There was no room. And yet, her body surrendered, the tight ring of muscle giving way as his cock slid deeply inside her. Once he was completely in, he paused letting her adjust to the feeling. The sensation of both of her husbands inside her body was amazing.

But she feared moving.

Clenching her muscles, she felt as if she were attacking and holding hostage both men. Both of their cocks stuffed inside her. Neither of them moved.

Taking a breath, she moaned as Daniel moved in farther, then retreated, the feel of him hard and thick and so wonderful.

"Oh, my," she said. "Both of you are now inside me. Fuck me."

A hot rush of desire raced through her. Pinned between them, she whimpered at how they controlled her completely. They began to move, and she gasped, crying out at the rush of feelings.

First, Daniel, then Alex, each pushing her closer and closer to the edge as they retreated and then filled her over and over. In and out, they maneuvered her body bringing them all to the brink of pleasure.

"Alex," she cried. "Daniel."

"Darling, just hang on," Alex said, his breathing heavy. "We're almost there."

Alex pounded into her with Daniel retreating. Between these two men was where she belonged. Here was her life. She needed the two of them to fuck her. To claim her. To make her theirs.

How could she live without them? They were her men and she loved them with all her heart and soul.

"Please, can I come?" she cried, knowing she couldn't hold out much longer.

"Oh, yes," Daniel gasped.

"Take my cock deep and squeeze it," Alex cried.

A scream tore through her throat as she squeezed and held her men, working the seed from their bodies. Nothing mattered, but her two men. They were hers and she was theirs.

First, Daniel and then Alex came, their seed coating her insides, as they held her between them, their cocks buried deep within her. Her breathing was heavy as her heartbeat slowed, and she loved being sandwiched between them.

Nothing else mattered but these two men. They were her world, her center of the universe, and tonight the Indian princess and warrior had saved her. That had to be a sign.

No barriers remained between them. Tonight, her men had marked her, made her theirs. Joy filled her at the thought of their long life together. Hopefully, soon, they would have a baby.

Breathing heavily, they reluctantly pulled free from her, but held her between them. This was where she belonged. This was her life. Her life with her husbands was perfect in every sense of the word as long as the bank in South Carolina dropped the charges.

"I love both of you," she whispered as she lay between them. "You rescued me from danger and gave me the life I wanted. Thank you."

They rose and loomed over her, each man leaning on his elbow.

"Darling, you are the one who made our life perfect," Daniel said. "I didn't want to marry until you."

Alex smiled. "This is so much more than I dreamed of. Thank you, Francis. Thank you for loving us."

She grinned and then gazed at her husbands. "As soon as you're ready. I'm ready to go again."

CHAPTER 23

One year later, Alex and Daniel paced outside the bedroom door. Every so often, Alex would peek in and then his face would turn white and he'd step away.

"No baby yet," he said.

"I'm going in," Daniel said. "I want to see my son born."

Alex shook his head, his body giving a little shiver. "Not me. You go."

Daniel opened the door just as Aunt Grace encouraged Francis. "Push. You're almost done."

She gazed at him and screamed as she bore down.

"Good girl," the doctor said. "The baby is coming."

"Daniel Smith, if you ever get me pregnant again, I will kill you," she promised as she panted.

"Darling, we said we wanted a big family," he told her still having reservations about his background. All he could do was hope and pray his children weren't spawns of the devil like the James gang, but rather more like their mother.

"One more time," the doctor said. "His head is crowning."

She glared at him and pushed once again.

And then a rush of emotion came over Daniel as the baby, a boy came out screaming bloody murder. His son.

"Welcome to the world, son," the doctor said as he began to check the child. Then he reached up and began to push on Francis's stomach.

"Wait a minute," he said, his eyes growing wide. "I think we've got another baby."

"What?"

"I'm sorry you're going to have to push again," the doctor said.

Aunt Grace took Francis's hand. "Twins. How exciting. Come on, you can do it again."

"I can't," she cried. "I'm tired."

Daniel walked over to her side. "Darling, I love you. For me and Alex, please this one might be that girl you're wanting."

Tears rolled down her cheeks and her bottom lip trembled.

"Push," the doctor ordered.

"If you want to scream at me, go ahead," Daniel said. "For you and our babies, I'll take the abuse."

Francis opened her mouth and screamed, clamping down on his hand as she gave it her all and pushed.

The doctor laughed as the baby popped out. "A girl. You have a boy and a girl."

"Twins," Aunt Grace said. "Congratulations."

The little girl glanced up at them and gave a little mewl. Then the doctor patted her on the back and she squealed like her brother.

Just then Alex walked into the room. "What's happened?"

"Twins," Daniel told him. "We have twins. A boy and a girl."

Alex saw the amount of blood and suddenly his legs buckled beneath him and he passed out.

Daniel couldn't help but laugh.

Aunt Grace had cleaned the little boy and she placed him in Daniel's arms. Gazing down at his son, tears welled in his eyes.

How could he not have wanted a child?

"I promise to do my best by you," he told the infant who gazed at him and then yawned. "You and your sister and any brothers and sisters you have. We're your parents and we're going to love you all your life. Just don't let your family history cloud your judgment."

He walked over to the bed, where Francis lay back exhausted.

"Meet our son," he said, placing him in her arms.

Smiling at him, she gazed down at the baby. "He's so tiny."

"Yes, he is," Daniel said.

Just then Alex moaned and sat up on the floor.

"Did you say twins?"

"Yes, I did. Come meet your son," Daniel told the man.

Aunt Grace stepped to his side of Francis's bed. "Here is the little girl. I'm so excited for you."

The baby glanced up at them as if she was trying to understand who they were.

Alex leaned over the bed and kissed Francis. "Thank you, darling. You did good."

She smiled. "No, we did good. Now tell me, what are we going to name these two?"

"Can we name the daughter after my mother, Sara?" Alex asked.

Francis smiled and nodded.

"And I'd like to name the boy after your father," Daniel said to Francis. "You said he was killed by some marauders."

Francis gasped and the tears rolled down her cheeks. "I love that idea. Thank you, my husbands. My life is complete because of you."

THANKS FOR READING Our Dangerous Bride. I love writing these stories and I hope you enjoy them as well. I would love it if you would leave me a review. In the meantime, here is a sneak preview of Our Lucky Bride.

PEARL TUTTLE LOVED TO GAMBLE. And most of the time she was very successful. But for the last month, she'd lost every time she played. She'd lost to the point she owed the Charleston Gambling Hall over two thousand dollars.

Tonight she entered the hall and glanced around, trying to decide which table would be her lucky one where could she make back the money she owed.

"Miss Tuttle, Mr. Wiggins would like to see you in his office," the dealer told her.

"What for?"

"I have no idea, ma'am," he said not looking at her.

A shiver went up her spine. She was broke. Penniless. Barely surviving.

Now she feared they wanted their money back. And no matter how much she played, her luck had not changed for the better.

"I'll take you to his office," he said as another gentleman stepped up to take his place as the dealer.

The tables were loaded with wealthy men and even some poor men trying to make money.

They walked up the elegant stairs into the area of the gambling hall known for housing women. She'd never been up here before and her stomach tightened in knots. What could they do to her? She'd already lost her plantation home to carpetbaggers and she had survived on what little money was left from her papa's accounts and gambling.

Until her run of bad luck. She would need to find a husband or some kind of job very soon.

The man knocked on a large wooden door.

"Come in," a deep voice called.

He opened the door and then shut it behind her.

"Miss Tuttle," a finely dressed man said, standing and

taking her hand. "James Wiggins, owner of this establishment."

"Nice to meet you," he said.

"This is Miss Champe," he said. "She runs the bordello side of our establishment."

Pearl licked her lips, her nerves tightening like a vise in her chest. What was she doing here?

The woman was dressed even fancier than Mr. Wiggins. What did they want with her?

"It's come to my attention that you owe the house more than two thousand dollars."

"I've borrowed two thousand is all," she said.

"But with interest, it's now almost three thousand dollars," he said with a grin.

"What? That's outrageous. It's only been a couple of weeks."

"No one said borrowing money from the gambling saloon was cheap. We make it quite expensive to keep our gamblers from not paying us. In your case, you have no way of paying it back. So I'm calling the note due right now. Can you pay us back?"

Her stomach clenched. Why had she borrowed from him? She had been doing so well and then suddenly her luck just dried up. Suddenly it was as if every hand the dealer won.

"No, I can't pay it all back at once. I was planning on paying it back a little at a time."

"At thirty percent interest, it's going to take you years to pay us back," he said, grinning at her. "So I sold the note to Miss Champe. She now has your debt."

Why in the world would this woman want to hold her debt?

"I'm calling the loan due. Since you are unable to pay it back in full right now, you will now be required to work for the brothel. Are you a virgin?"

Stunned, she stared at the woman, horror filling her. She'd seen the women about in the gambling hall. She'd seen the kind of men they took upstairs and she wanted nothing to do with this. And yet what choice did she have?

"That is none of your business."

Just then a man entered the room.

"Strip," Miss Champe said.

"What? No, I'm not disrobing here in front of these men."

The lady grinned and held up a flogger with leather strands that had a knot on the end. She banged it against Mr. Wiggins's desk.

"I said strip or I will use this on you right now."

The man behind her leaned down and whispered in her ear.

"I need to examine you," he said.

"Do it now," the woman screamed at her as she moved toward her. "I do not accept intolerance from my girls. You will obey me or you will face the flogger."

Swallowing her tears, Pearl stood. She began to unbutton the front of her bodice. Dragging it out as long as possible, she stepped out of her dress.

"Remove everything," the woman said. "We want to see what we have to work with."

They were going to make her into a whore. What had she done?

Slowly, she removed her petticoats and corset until she was down to her shift.

"I'm tired of waiting on you," the woman said and she reached out and ripped the material off her, exposing her to the men in the room.

Quickly she tried to cover herself with her hands.

"Oh, stop it," the woman said. "Soon many men will see you. Now lie back on the table."

"Why?"

"Dr. Reed is going to make certain you're a virgin," she said.

The man helped her onto the desk and then he went down between her legs. She'd never felt so embarrassed in all her life. Tears welled in her eyes and then she felt his fingers going up inside her womanly area.

A sob escaped her.

"Yes, she's a virgin," he said, removing his hands and standing back.

Mr. Wiggns glanced at Miss Champe and grinned. "You could make most of your money back on the auction."

"My interest is a bit higher. She will have to work one year in the brothel to pay off her debts. By that time, she'll be soiled goods and no man will want to marry her, so most of my girls stay."

One year of her life being a prostitute?

No!

The madam walked over to her and swatted her with the flogger.

Her legs stung where she hit her. What would her life be like with this woman? Hell was all she could think of.

"Don't even think about running away. I will find you. I will allow you to return to your boarding house and pack your things. One of my men will accompany you and bring you back here as soon as you finish packing. Don't delay, it will only make me angry and you'll feel the flogger again."

"Damn shame she's a virgin. I would have liked a little sample," Mr. Wiggins said.

Pearl sat up and started to put her clothes on, not waiting to be told.

"You can have seconds," Miss Champe said. "We'll hold the auction on Friday night and I expect her to be very busy that night."

The man reached out and tried to grab her breast, but she moved out of his reach and quickly put her chemise on. She'd never been so humiliated.

The madam walked to the door. "George," she called.

A big burly man walked to the door just as she finished dressing. Did these people not have any shame?

"Take Miss Tuttle to her boarding house to pack her belongings. Stand outside her door and do not let her escape. Make certain she gets back here within the hour."

"Yes, ma'am," he said.

"She's going to be one of the new girls. If she escapes you will be punished."

Pearl wiped her eyes, grabbed her reticule, and made for

the door. She was going to do her best to escape from the hellish life they had planned for her.

"Pearl, don't try to escape or you will be punished. I'd hate to auction you off with your ass striped. Do you understand?"

"Yes," she said not looking at the woman, knowing she had to make an attempt to save herself.

"I expect you back here in one hour," she said. "Now, get going."

It was all Pearl could do not to spit at the woman, but that would only get her another beating.

"Welcome to the family, Pearl," Mr. Wiggins said, laughing. "I can't wait to fuck you."

Without a word, she hurried out the door, her eyes swimming with tears. Her love of gambling had ruined her. Somehow she had to escape.

Available at Your Favorite Retailer

The Gambler Takes a Chance on Treasure Falls

Peart Tuttle is the slyest gambler in town. For the last two years, she has survived on her own by making enough money to keep her from going broke. But now her gambler's luck has run out and she owes the saloon a hefty sum. Time to join the mail-order brides and get out of town.

Widower Anthony Sanders owns a ranch in Treasure Falls and believes he will never love again. Yet, he wants children to pass his land to. Wesley Pickens has led a reckless life and only recently with Tony's help has managed to stay out of trouble. Would a woman settle him down or will the bad boy return to his wild ways?

Can Pearl escape her debts or will the past make her pay up in her new hometown? Will Tony and Wesley put their histories behind them or will Pearl become the abandoned bride of Treasure Falls?

PLEASE LEAVE A REVIEW

Did you enjoy the book? Reviews help authors. I would appreciate you posting a review.

Follow Lacey Davis on Facebook.

Sign up for my New Book Alert at my website www.Laceydavisauthor.com and receive a free book.

OUR CHRISTMAS BRIDE

The stagecoach bounced along the road, past the pine trees and the mountains in the distance, carrying Carrie Sanders home. She was returning as an abject failure, but she no longer cared.

She was tired of hiding her life and family ways and trying to fit in with those fancy girls in her finishing school. She was done and heading home to Treasure Falls. Time to begin life. The life she longed for.

Her brothers be damned. They didn't rule her. For too long, she'd let her brothers control her and that was in the past. At eighteen, she could do what she wanted, and she'd been homesick for the past two years.

Enough. Time to go home, take a stand, and find her place in their community. It was what their parents would've wanted her to do even though there would be a shitstorm on the horizon.

The stage rounded the last curve and she took a deep

breath of the mountain air. It felt so good to be back in Montana – the colder air, open spaces, and the mountaintops already sporting a white coat promising winter was on the way.

She had escaped the stifling city life with women who lifted their noses into the air as they passed her by. According to those "fine" women, she was an abomination.

She was the product of a two-husband family, only thing was both her two fathers and her mother had died in the mining accident. So she knew firsthand the importance of having two husbands.

In Treasure Falls, as the founder of the town, her family was one of the most respected, but she had never concerned herself with being upper-crust society. What did that mean? That your family had a little more money?

All that mattered was the sense of belonging she missed. Treasure Falls was home and it was time to leave the snobs behind in Denver where they belonged. Time for this abomination to return to where she felt loved and wanted.

Who knew that having two husbands was such a banned or taboo subject? She had certainly created a stir when she told them that her mother had two husbands. Her aunt had two husbands, and even her brothers were married to a woman they shared with another man.

By the girls' overreactions, you would have thought her family were sexual deviants holding wild orgies and not the family life they enjoyed. Not the pledge to protect one another and stand beside each other.

They didn't understand what happened to a woman alone with a family to raise when her husband died.

In the city, the dangers were not as evident as they were here. Bear attacks, mining collapses, cougar attacks, Treasure Falls had it all, even blizzards. Here, the chances of becoming a young widow were high. With an additional husband, the family would be protected. This way a woman would not be without someone to take care of her and the children.

And her family had sacrificed a lot for this little town. Including the lives of her two fathers and her mother. The memory of that stressful time hung like a cloud over her until her brothers sent her away to that fancy finishing school with the intent that she would marry into high society.

High society be damned too. She didn't like those uppity men or snooty women. That was not the life for her.

Wouldn't her brothers be shocked when they learned she had traveled all this way by herself?

No one knew she was returning. No one would be waiting at the stage depot. Her arrival would be a huge surprise to everyone.

The last few months had been filled with exciting adventures that had her changing the course of her life. Had her returning to her roots.

"Treasure Falls," the driver called as he pulled the horses to a stop.

Home, she was home and couldn't wait to see her aunt Grace and Doc Owen.

She sat patiently inside the coach for the driver to put the stool down and open the door. When the handle turned, she jumped up, eager to get out of this rattletrap she'd spent days bouncing inside of.

Stepping out of the stage, she gazed about at the town she loved. The place that held all her fond memories of her mother and fathers and even her brothers before they became her caretakers.

Before they decided to rule her life.

Though it had only been a couple years, the town had grown. It appeared they now had a small cafe.

She laughed, feeling relieved to be back. "Thank you," she said to the driver. "Have a safe trip home."

"Yes, ma'am," he said. "What do you want me to do with your trunk?"

There was no way she could carry the thing. And she hated going off and leaving it just sitting, but what choice did she have?

"Leave it," she said. "I'll have someone take it home for me."

"All right," he told her.

The luggage would be safe sitting there for ten minutes. It would take her five minutes to walk to Aunt Grace's home, and after they said hello, she was certain a servant could come fetch it for her.

Leaves blew along the street as she walked toward the house where she had grown up. The same house that once belonged to her parents before they were killed. Now the doctor and her aunt lived in the big home.

A cold wind howled out of the north and she huddled into her coat. She was fortunate to have made it home. Another week and the trails would be impassable. But once the headmistress kicked her out, she didn't tarry. She'd taken the first stage home.

It was something she should have done months ago. At the first signs of her receiving the society snub, she should have packed her bags and told those rich bitches she was going searching for her two husbands. Wouldn't that have set them off in a tizzy?

With a giggle, she hurried up the street, remembering playing along this avenue as a child. Things were about to get interesting.

After running up the steps to the house, she knocked on the large wooden door. The house looked the same, only a little more weather-worn. Montana winters were hard on the wooden structures.

Her aunt opened the door, her sapphire eyes growing large, and she couldn't get the door opened fast enough.

"Carrie," she cried, "what are you doing here?"

"I've come home," she said as her aunt threw open the door and wrapped her arms around her. "That fancy school didn't want a girl who believed in more than one husband."

Her aunt hugged her tightly, and it brought tears to her eyes. She was tired of feeling like an outcast. Here in her aunt's arms, she felt reassured that she'd made the right decision.

This was home.

"Oh, darling, I'm so happy to see you. It was long past time for you to come home. Where are you staying?"

Carrie giggled as her aunt stepped back. "I don't know. No one knows I'm here but you."

"You didn't tell your brothers?" she asked, shocked.

"No, I knew they would try to convince me to stay and I couldn't for one more minute."

"You're right," her aunt said. "Stay here with us. You can have your old bedroom back. We'd love to have you. You know your brothers have all married."

"Oh, yes," she said. "That's why I didn't know where I was going to sleep. Nothing is the same since the accident."

"No, it's not," her aunt agreed sadly.

The thought of staying in her old bedroom brought warmth to her chest. Tears welled in her eyes. "I've been so homesick."

"Well, then, it's fitting you stay here with us. Where is your trunk?"

"Down at the station," she said. "I couldn't carry it."

"Of course not," her aunt said. "I'll get Henry to fetch it for you."

Just then she remembered her mother's jewelry was in the trunk and it wasn't locked. "I need to get back to my luggage. Tell Henry to meet me at the station."

The heirloom jewelry was the only thing she had of her mother and she wasn't about to let someone take those few precious pieces. They weren't worth a lot, but their sentimental value was worth millions.

"I'll fix a warm pot of tea and have it waiting for you. You go and I'll send Henry."

Carrie stared at her aunt, tears filling her eyes. The elder had grown older, her hair almost completely gray. She wondered how her mother would have looked at this age. So many times, Carrie yearned to hear her parents' voices.

"I've missed you so much," she said.

Her aunt reached out and hugged her again. "Darling, it's so good to have you home. Now get back there and gather your things. Then we can catch up when you return. You can tell me all about how this finishing school decided you no longer needed to be there."

Carrie chuckled. It was quite the story. People who didn't know about Treasure Falls's way of life had no idea what a great family town it was. Their loss.

One thing she'd learned in the past two years, her fists could get her into trouble. Because no one spoke badly of her family and their beliefs. No one. She protected those she loved.

And now she was home. It was only a matter of time before her brothers learned she was here and then the explosions would commence.

Didn't matter, she wasn't going back, and since today was the last stage coming into Treasure Falls, they couldn't make her return.

Available at Your Favorite Retailer
The Princess and the Paupers

Carrie Spencer grew up in Treasure Falls with two fathers. When her parents were killed in a mining accident, she learned exactly why two husbands were essential. Now she's grown and ready for two men of her own. But there are no eligible men in Treasure Falls.

Levi Daly and Jasper Vanderbilt have traveled the world, made their fortune, and now want to return home. No longer are Levi and Jasper two poor kids, living on the wrong side of Main Street. No longer are they not good enough to marry a Spencer, or so Levi believes. He has loved Carrie since they were children, but Jasper and she were childhood enemies.

Can Levi convince Carrie to marry him and Jasper? Or will they continue to be enemies? Can the poor kids marry the town's favored daughter?

Treasure Falls Brides Box Set 1-3
Treasure Falls Brides Box Set 4-6

Want to learn about my new releases before anyone else? Sign up for my New Book Alert and receive a complimentary book. Blindfold Me.

ABOUT THE AUTHOR

Lacey Davis is a pseudonym for a USA Today bestselling author who wanted to try her hand at writing sexy romance. With these novels, I hope to write sizzling romances that will leave you grabbing a fan to cool yourself off.

If you like hunky bad boy heroes who like to be in charge and strong pretty women who are willing to risk it all, then look no further. These sexy reads will get you in the mood. Come experience strong women who will tame these bad boys and leave them wanting more.

www.LaceyDavisauthor.com
The End